TANNER: FIREBRAND COWBOYS

BARB HAN

TORJAKE PUBLISHING

Copyright © 2023 by Barb Han

All rights reserved.

No part of this book may be reproduced in any form or by any electronic or mechanical means, including information storage and retrieval systems, without written permission from the author, except for the use of brief quotations in a book review.

Editing: Ali Williams

Cover Design: Jacob's Cover Designs

Proofreading: Judicious Revisions

To Brandon, Jacob, and Tori for being the great loves of my life. To Babe for being my hero, my best friend, and my place to call home.

1

A bolt of lightning stretched across the night sky, like long tentacles gripping the once-velvet canopy, in search of something just out of reach. The dotting of stars was now fully covered by rolling gray clouds—clouds that had an ominous feel. The weatherman warned tonight's storm could bring hail and possible tornadoes, derailing the search team's efforts.

The search is being called for tonight.

Like hell it was. There wasn't a thunderstorm strong enough to stop Tanner Firebrand from searching for his missing friend; text or no text from the lead volunteer. BethAnne Dyer was out here somewhere. He could feel it in his bones.

This stretch of land near the water was on the boundary of the Guadalupe River State Park. Tree branches along the bank looked like a thick, tangled web. Hiking and camping were popular along this four-mile stretch of river. BethAnne hiking or camping, though? It's not something Tanner would have guessed in a million years. Something wasn't right.

A pair of volunteers twenty feet ahead stopped and stared at the ground on the other side of a rock. One of them knelt down. Tanner's heart skipped a beat. The reality that this was about to go from a search and rescue to a search and recover mission struck like a physical blow; the volunteer stood and shook his head. BethAnne had been missing forty-eight hours already. Time was the enemy.

The couple linked their hands and then turned toward the path leading to the parking lot, no doubt giving up for the night. Or maybe they were giving up on finding BethAnne altogether.

A few large droplets of rain spilled down from the swirling cloud overhead. One splatted on Tanner's forehead. It had the force of Ms. Wriggle's finger from fifth grade, when she poked Tanner for 'not trying.' A school counselor didn't figure out his dyslexia for another four years. Ninth grade was too little, too late for intervention, but Tanner's determination to read on the same level of his peers kept him up late nights studying, attempting to catch up.

Tanner Firebrand didn't give up, which was the reason he planned to stay the night in the small tent he'd set up, just in case BethAnne came this way in need of immediate assistance on the way to her car parked in the lot. Her cell must have fallen out of her purse or backpack next to her vehicle without her realizing it. Tracking software had given the sheriff the location of her cell after she'd texted her cousin about being 'out of pocket' for a couple of days to go camping.

"Are you heading out too?" a somewhat familiar female voice cut through the howling winds from behind.

He turned to answer. Did he know the tall, wheat-colored blond? "I'm here for the night. How about you?"

"Tanner?" She took a couple of steps toward him, squinting as rain pelted them both. "Is that you?"

She knew him? Hold on a minute. Recognition dawned. He knew exactly who this was. "Aimee Anderson. It's been a long time."

The wind whipped her hair around. She brought a hand up to hold it back from her face. "It has. I don't get to Lone Star Pass much anymore. Not since middle school. My cousin preferred to come to Austin to visit me. Said we'd done everything there was to do in Lone Star Pass by the time I was nine."

Aimee was four years younger than Tanner and BethAnne, who'd been in the same grade in school.

"I'm sorry about BethAnne," he said, raising his voice to compete with the howling winds. "We won't stop until we find her." He stopped short of saying *alive,* although that was still the hope.

Aimee gave a slight nod of acknowledgment. Her chin quivered as she tucked it to her chest and then turned her face away from him before clearing her throat. "Thank you." Shoulders straight, she took in a breath and faced him again. "Looks like everyone else is going home for the night."

"Keith and Travis are still here," he pointed out, having to shout over the winds. "Not everyone intends to call it a day."

"That means a lot, Tanner. I'm sure my cousin appreciates the support from you and your family."

Aimee spoke about BethAnne in the present tense. Good. She hadn't given up on finding her cousin alive.

The conditions, however, were getting worse fast, which might mean the storm would blow over just as quickly. "Do you want to get out of the rain? My tent isn't far from here."

"Okay," she said, both hands trying to keep her long hair from slapping her in the face. She managed to wrangle most of her thick locks into a rubber band that she pulled from her wrist as she followed him to higher ground where he'd staked his dome tent.

After unzipping the door, he let her go inside first.

"I can hear myself think in here," she said, sitting down and crossing her legs like they'd done during circle time in elementary school. Rain dripped down her face. Her hair and clothing were wet.

Tanner pulled out a hand towel from his supply bag. "It isn't much, but it'll help."

Aimee thanked him after taking the offering. She patted her face and neck before wringing her hair into the towel. She was four years younger than him and BethAnne, so he hadn't paid much attention to her looks back when he was in high school. Now? They were impossible to ignore. The thickest, blackest pair of eyelashes hooded cobalt blue eyes, contrasting against her creamy skin. Her pink, kissable lips weren't something he should be staring at, so he lifted his gaze to those eyes, causing his heart to skip another beat for a different reason this time. She was tall, all legs, with a lean runner's build and just enough curves to make her sexy. More facts he didn't need to notice about her under the circumstances.

She handed over the towel. "That's a big help, actually."

"There's not much I can do about your wet clothes," he said, taking the offering and redirecting his thoughts away from how much she'd changed and grown up. "I have no magic there."

"It's not like her." Aimee lifted her gaze to meet his. "She's not a hiker or a camper."

"I was just thinking the same thing before I ran into you."

"She texted me to say she was doing it, though," Aimee continued on a shrug. "Never answered when I asked what the hell she was thinking."

"Did she mention coming here with someone?" It was the only logical thing in his mind. BethAnne wouldn't do this by herself.

Aimee shook her head. "I immediately assumed she was meeting up with someone and she wasn't ready to talk about him."

"As in a new relationship?" It would explain why she hadn't been seen around town with anyone.

"That's where my mind went," she admitted. "You know how it is when you first meet someone and you're putting your best foot forward? If they want to go camping, you go camping. If they like a band, you'll try listening to it."

"Until the shine wears off a new relationship and folks settle back into who they really are." He knew the pattern all too well. It's how he'd lost most of his girlfriends. They thought ranching life was fun until they realized it wasn't just horseback riding and picturesque hayrides. "That's when the relationship usually ends."

Aimee nodded as she shot him a look that told him she'd been down the same road. "Funny how they think your habits and routines are cute until you don't change up your life to suit theirs. Then, all of a sudden, they get in the way and become a nuisance."

"I'm far too stubborn to change on someone else's whim." Which explained why he was still single and dedicated to the cause. Although he could admit ever since he turned thirty a year ago, it felt like something was missing in his life.

Even so, he'd be damned if he fell into the trap of thinking someone else could fill it; Tanner had everything he needed, except perhaps a dog. As much as he enjoyed the animals on the ranch, like Hutch and Miss Peabody, to name a few, he was ready for the companionship of a dog of his own.

Relationships were too unpredictable. Speaking of which, he had a thought pertaining to BethAnne.

"An investigation into phone records and e-mails should reveal if your cousin was seeing someone," Tanner said, breaking into Aimee's thoughts. She'd forgotten how good-looking the Firebrand men were. Tanner was no exception. In her opinion, he stood far above the rest, which was saying something. And she'd had a small crush on him years ago that seemed to still be simmering.

"The sheriff has been cooperative so far, but information is flowing one way right now," she revealed. "He hasn't been too keen on telling me anything."

"Right now, she is considered 'missing' and could be of her own accord," he pointed out. "In theory, at least. There's no reason to suggest foul play since her phone was found in the parking lot right where she said she was going."

"She should have surfaced by now, though."

"He has to consider the possibility she doesn't want to be found," he said. "If she hadn't let you know where she was going, he would probably be more worried."

"He said something along those lines." She still didn't believe her cousin would go camping and then disappear for two solid days without making contact. "Her car is in the parking lot. Her phone was found underneath it, like you already mentioned. She's missing. What else is there? Why isn't he connecting the dots?"

"There was no sign of struggle in the parking lot, for one."

Why did he have to make so much sense when she was running on pure emotion? "That's true."

"It might not be characteristic of BethAnne, but it's realistic to think she happened to lose her phone before going camping with or without someone else," he said. Again, making more sense than she wanted to hear.

"I know," she conceded. "But do you ever just get a feeling in your bones that tells you something is dead wrong? That someone you love is in trouble?"

"Yes, I do."

"Then, you know what I'm talking about."

"It's the reason I'm here in the first place and the reason I'm not leaving until we find her, find Aimee."

"Same," was all she said. All she needed to say to the handsome rancher. He'd been four years older than her at school, and way out of her league, despite the crush she'd had on him. He'd been BethAnne's friend so, therefore, off limits anyway. Not that he'd looked twice at Aimee all those years ago when she'd visited Lone Star Pass to spend time with her cousin.

It was all water under the bridge now.

BethAnne might be Aimee's cousin, but she felt more like a big sister. "Did you know BethAnne was the first one in our family to go to college?"

Tanner shook his head.

"She was," Aimee explained as rain pelted the tent. "In fact, she was the one who inspired me to get a degree, which wasn't easy. I had to work two jobs just to afford classes, because I had to pitch in to help my mom with rent.

She did her best, but couldn't afford to do everything on her own."

"I remember BethAnne moving back to Lone Star Pass after college," he said with a smile that warmed Aimee's heart. She liked being able to talk to someone else who cared about her cousin.

"Why didn't the two of you ever date?" The question came out before she could reel it in, no matter how much she wished she could do just that at the moment. "Sorry. You don't have to answer that."

Tanner's cheeks turned red. "It's fine. We had a great friendship and decided a long time ago that we would have ruined it by dating. Good friends are hard to come by. Plus, I'm related to half the town." He chuckled. "BethAnne and I made a pact in ninth grade never to cross that line, so we could be in each other's lives forever."

"That might be the sweetest thing I've ever heard," she admitted, knowing full well BethAnne's heart was not in the pact all those years ago. She might have resigned herself to the fact Tanner wouldn't go there. He was known to dig his heels in.

"I'm surprised she never told you, considering how close the two of you were," he said with an arched brow.

"I asked outright one time and she got flustered." If Aimee had to guess, she would say the friendship pact only lasted on one side. "I'm pretty sure she had a crush on you all through middle and high school."

"I doubt it," he said. "We'd made the pact long before senior year."

People changed. Aimee had loads of personal experience to draw from there. Her own mother had turned on her after meeting Aimee's now stepfather. At least, stepfather by common law marriage guidelines. Old folks had used the term, *shacking up,* to describe Rena and Jack's relationship status. Her mother liked the words, *it's complicated.*

The only thing complicated about Rena now was the strained relationship with her only child. But then, the writing had been on the wall for that one for quite a lot of years. Aimee had chosen to see what she wanted their bond to be over what it had become. A lost cause.

"What about you?" Tanner's voice broke through her heavy thoughts. She looked over in time to see him glance at her wedding ring finger.

"Oh, God, no," she said. "I need a man in my life like I need needles in my eyes."

His stunned reaction made her laugh.

"That was graphic," she said. "I didn't mean it to sound like that."

His eyebrow shot up again. "Sounds like there's a story behind those words."

"Not really," she said, rolling her shoulders a couple of times to work off some of the tension. "I've just never been one of those people who needed someone in their life to feel complete, which goes against popular romantic ideas."

"Not to me, it doesn't."

A kindred spirit?

"Plus, I've watched my mother's relationships over the years." She involuntarily shivered. "No, thanks."

He outright laughed, causing her stomach to flip and heat to rush through her.

Aimee reminded herself she was in the presence of a Firebrand. Someone who probably had chemistry with a whole lot of ladies. Except that he didn't strike her as a player who went around sleeping with women and ditching them straight after. Not to mention the fact BethAnne wouldn't get close to someone like that anyway. She'd only ever spoken about Tanner in the best possible light. He'd reached something close to saint status with her cousin.

The real person was likely somewhere in between saint and sinner in the gray area where most spent their lives.

Aimee's cell buzzed at the same time as Tanner's. The odds of that happening randomly weren't high, which caused an ominous feeling to settle over her. She searched for her phone inside her small backpack-style purse as he fished it out of his front pocket. The fact he cursed after checking the screen sent her pulse through the roof.

Aimee's hand shook as her fingers closed around her phone. She checked the screen.

Three words sucked the air out of the tent. Aimee struggled to take in a breath as anger roared through her. The message could only mean one thing…BethAnne was dead.

"I'm going right now."

Tanner shook his head. "Not a good idea."

"Doesn't matter," she countered as the urge to scream became a physical ache.

Tanner looked resigned. "Whatever we walk up on, we'll face it together."

As much as she might be reassured by his presence, he couldn't fix this. He couldn't erase the three words on the screen.

She's been found.

2

BethAnne was buried in a shallow grave, her mouth sewn shut.

Tanner stood in between the sheriff and Aimee, who'd turned to puke, doing his best to hold his stomach contents in. "This might be my fault."

"What makes you say something like that?" Sheriff Lawler asked. Timothy Lawler had been two grades ahead of Tanner's cousin Adam in school. The sheriff had been a star quarterback who'd been scouted by several big-name programs until he took a hit that broke his arm in four places, ending his dreams of playing college ball.

"The mouth…"

He stopped as bile burned the back of his throat. Seeing BethAnne like this would haunt him for the rest of his life. It was bad enough that his friend was gone. But to be taken out in this manner, with such obvious hostility, caused his hands to fist at his sides.

"Yeah?" Lawler was one of the good guys. His ginger hair was always cut tight, military style. A hawk-like nose sat below a pair of compassionate brown eyes. He wore jeans, boots, and a tan shirt with the word, Sheriff, embroidered on the right front pocket, his usual.

"Hold on," Tanner said to Lawler, needing to make sure Aimee was okay. After seeing her cousin in this condition, okay might be too much to hope for. Not puking her insides out would be a more realistic hope. He placed his hand on her back as she bent over in the opposite direction, dry coughing. "Hey."

"I'm alright," she lied, he guessed she was putting up a brave front. "Keep talking so the bastard who did this doesn't get away."

Keeping one hand on her back to reassure her that he wasn't going anywhere, he turned toward the sheriff. The rain had stopped for the moment, but the storm promised to get a whole lot worse. "BethAnne told me a secret that might have upset someone enough to want to punish her. Alicia tried to trick my brother Rowan into thinking she was pregnant by him."

"Weren't BethAnne and Alicia friends?" Lawler asked.

"Yes, sir," Tanner replied. "BethAnne was too good of a person to let a lie like that go on, once she found out what Alicia had done."

"Alicia should have realized Rowan would ask for a paternity test."

"I highly doubt she thought it through, sir," Tanner continued. "But my brother had no reason to believe she'd cheated, since everything seemed fine between them. He'd been clear about not wanting a family or marriage, until he met someone in Colorado, that is."

"Tara Dowling."

"Yes, sir." Tanner forced himself to look at BethAnne, who was too still lying in the dirt half covered with it. He searched her limp body for clues as to who might have done this to her if not Alicia. Something wasn't adding up about the scene. "Alicia wouldn't have been able to carry BethAnne far, would she?"

"Not without help," the sheriff responded as he scanned the ground. He pointed. "The rain is washing away evidence as we speak, but it does look like one person pulled the deceased into the grave."

Tanner noticed Lawler didn't use BethAnne's name. Was it a way to keep emotional distance? Because Tanner could use a few tips as his emotions flooded him. Anger. There was an emotion. It was all-consuming at the moment. His hands fisted as a feeling of helplessness came over him like a heavy, gray rolling cloud on an otherwise sunny day. He clenched his back teeth so hard they might crack as he kept his gaze on BethAnne. "This isn't deep, so I doubt they dug this in advance."

Lawler nodded. "Families frequent this area and kids are generally given a wide berth of freedom if they're old enough to handle it. Whoever chose this sight would know this, in the event this was planned in advance."

"Would someone do this to another person if it wasn't pre-meditated?" Tanner motioned toward her mouth.

"Not likely," the sheriff confirmed.

"Which means this was planned in advance," Tanner stated.

Lawler held a hand up to stop Tanner from continuing down that path. "Right now, we don't know that. It's too early to make assumptions, so let's hold off as I gather evidence and interview folks."

Tanner seethed. "The person who did this shouldn't be allowed to sleep in their own bed tonight. BethAnne was a kind person with a heart of gold. She didn't deserve this."

His anger took the wheel again. He had to remind himself to slow down and breathe.

"I can see why your mind would go to Alicia," Lawler said sympathetically. "It's one trail." He paused for a few beats. "There will be others. In my experience, cases like these are rarely so cut and dried. I have to look at this from all angles. Believe me when I say the person responsible might get to sleep in their bed tonight or even a few more. But justice will be served." He turned to Tanner. "Which means the legal system, not a vigilante."

The thought had crossed Tanner's mind. He clamped his mouth shut rather than give away the fact he'd been seriously contemplating taking matters into his own hands. "I plan to confront Alicia."

"Bad idea," Lawler said.

"Tell me why."

"Because you could scare her into lawyering up, for one," Lawler started, making logical sense when Tanner was working off pure emotion. "She is a suspect at this point, nothing more. There will be others. The more I can get her to think I'm asking her to cooperate, rather than pointing a finger at her, the better chance I have of getting her to talk to me and possibly incriminate herself."

Tanner put his fists on his hips. He scanned the area.

"I need your word that you won't interfere with my investigation, Tanner."

He issued a sharp sigh. "You have it." Which didn't mean Tanner wouldn't dig around or rattle some cages to get answers. But he gave his word that he wouldn't get in Lawler's way.

Aimee stood up, keeping her back to the makeshift grave. She'd seen more than enough and he didn't blame her for looking the other way. If he could do the same, he would. Guilt kept him from it. That same guilt would keep him from sleeping tonight, tomorrow night, and every night until the person responsible for BethAnne's murder was locked behind bars where they belonged.

"Why don't you take Ms. Anderson down to my office," Lawler offered. "Both of you can give statements there."

Tanner understood the sheriff's move. He was trying to get her away from her cousin's body and from the horror of what had just happened.

Aimee shook her head. "No, thank you, Sheriff." She turned to face the gravesite. "I'm not leaving her here alone."

"She won't be," Lawler said with compassion. The winds calmed down some and it was only drizzling now. A temporary reprieve? "I give you my word."

"As much as I believe you mean that, Sheriff, I have to decline the offer." She wiped a hand over her mouth and he noticed how much hers trembled. "I'm not leaving until she does."

The sheriff looked like he knew when he'd lost an argument. "Yes, ma'am. Let's start with you positively identifying the victim."

"That's my cousin BethAnne Dyer."

"Please provide your full name for the record." Lawler had pulled a small notebook and pencil from his pocket. He started scribbling on the pad before looking up and straight into Aimee's eyes, giving his full attention.

"Aimee Anderson," she said, rubbing her arms as she shivered.

Tanner shrugged out of his jacket and then wrapped it around her shoulders.

"You'll freeze," Aimee said, trying to give it back.

"I'm fine," he said, but knew he would never be fine

again until the person responsible for BethAnne's death had been found.

~

AIMEE SWALLOWED to ease the burn in the back of her throat. She reached in her purse for a peppermint, thinking she couldn't wait to take off the clothes she was wearing and burn them. She would never be able to put on these jeans without thinking of this day—a day that would end up on repeat far too many times in her mind already.

"Did your cousin have a boyfriend?" Lawler asked. Hearing him talk about BethAnne in the past tense gutted Aimee. She just wasn't there yet despite the evidence in front of her.

"Not that I know of," Aimee supplied, cluing back into the conversation. "Plus, I can't think of one reason she would go hiking or camping, since she was more of a lunch and shopping person."

"What about any recent fights with friends or co-workers?" Lawler continued.

Aimee shook her head. "BethAnne had a smile for just about everyone. She was the talkative one in the family. Bubbly and bright were good words to describe her personality. My cousin loved being a nurse, especially working for an OB/GYN. She got along with everyone in the office."

"When was the last time you two communicated?" Lawler asked.

"That would be two days ago, right before she came to this place," Aimee supplied. Would a random person do this to someone they didn't know? She couldn't imagine they would. Sewing someone's mouth shut seemed like a personal move, full of hate. Her cousin was chatty and wasn't very good at keeping secrets. But then, if you knew BethAnne, you wouldn't tell her anything too personal, and definitely nothing you didn't want broadcast all over town. "Do you think it's possible someone she knew did this?"

"I'm not sure yet," Lawler supplied. He was being honest, but she didn't care for the answer. "You supplied information when you reported her missing, but I have to ask again. What did your cousin say to you and how did she communicate?"

"It was a text," Aimee reminded, pulling out her phone. "Said she was going hiking and hoped I was having a good day."

She pulled up their conversation and held out her phone so the sheriff could see. His gaze moved left to right as he read her response asking if BethAnne had slipped and hit her head. There was a funny gif with someone falling off a cliff. Looking at it now, Aimee felt awful. Why had she sent something so insensitive?

Because she'd had no idea how this was how things were going to turn out. That's why.

"She never responded to you," he said.

"She left me on 'read.' No text and no phone call either," Aimee added. "That was it. That was the last message I sent her. Someone falling off a cliff." She wasn't sure what she expected to happen after her admission. But when Tanner reached for her arm, and then gave a gentle squeeze, warmth flooded her. Knowing he'd been close with BethAnne gave Aimee more comfort.

A thought struck out of the blue. How was she going to tell her aunt and uncle?

"Will someone visit BethAnne's parents to deliver the news?" Aimee asked the sheriff.

"Yes, ma'am."

"I should be there when it happens," she said. Aunt Denise and Uncle Chuckie had been nothing but kind to Aimee during her visits. Granted, they weren't close now but that didn't stop her from having fond memories of them. BethAnne had hinted at trouble in their marriage over the last few months. This news most likely wasn't going to help matters. The horror of the way in which their daughter died would make the news even more difficult to accept. BethAnne's parents loved her.

They deserved to have family there when they were told.

"I noticed there was no sign of struggle at my cousin's car in the parking lot," Aimee stated, checking for the sheriff's reaction. He probably wasn't going to tell her much based on the fact his mouth clamped shut.

"There will be a full investigation into this case," he said in a monotone voice that said he'd gone on autopilot with his responses. "I have to ask you to trust me that I can do my job." He paused for a few moments as his expression took on an even more serious note. "As much as I don't want to say this, I can't have either of your interfering with my case. I'd hate to have to file obstruction of justice charges or a host of other possible violations depending on your next steps."

"We won't get in your way, Sheriff." It was a promise she could keep. There was no way on earth Aimee was backing off this investigation, though. She would give the sheriff a wide berth, but she knew her cousin better than he did. He had a process to follow, whereas Aimee didn't have to worry about protocol.

Another thought struck.

"Have there been other cases like this one?" she asked him. She put her hands up, palms out, in the surrender position. "I'm just wondering if there is a serial killer on the loose." It would make the method in which he or she had killed BethAnne make more sense.

"I can't discuss other cases, so please don't make a habit of asking," he said. "But it's the first thing my office will be looking into."

Okay, so he didn't know. Because based on what had happened to BethAnne, she was either killed over a secret, or there was a serial killer out there who wanted to silence women. Still, the voluntary hike didn't sit well with Aimee. Had someone lured her cousin out here? In that case, the perp had to have been someone BethAnne knew. A shiver rocked her at the thought someone familiar could do such a thing to another human being, let alone her beloved cousin.

"Was your cousin seeing anyone new?" the sheriff asked.

"No, sir. Not to my knowledge." She'd gone over this same line of thinking with Tanner in the tent. It made sense, though. "All I can tell you is that my cousin wasn't the hiking type, which I'm sure you picked up from our text exchange."

"Yes, I did." He took a note. "Had she been in a fight with anyone that you know of recently?"

"No," Aimee said. "But she never mentioned the situation with Alicia."

"Does that strike you as odd?" the sheriff asked.

"No, sir. Not really. BethAnne was a talker, but she kept conversations to surface level, if you know what I mean. She wanted to know how I was doing and if I was seeing anyone. She liked gossip and a few of those reality shows. But she really loved margaritas and Tex-Mex food, which she would come to Austin for quite a bit. We had a never-ending debate going about who had the best tacos, Torchy's or Velvet Taco." A rogue tear escaped at the memory, running down her cheek. More welled in her eyes, so she stopped talking long enough to draw in a breath and face reality.

BethAnne was really gone. There would be no more taco debates or margaritas with her cousin. No more discussions over who would make the best celebrity boyfriend, book boyfriend, or real boyfriend.

Suddenly, it felt as if the world opened and tried to swallow Aimee whole. How was she going to survive without the cousin who'd made every Christmas brighter? Whose laugh was contagious? Who made the world a better, more humane place just by being in it?

"I can't do this right now," Aimee said, sucking in a breath.

"Take all the time you need," Lawler said as Tanner ushered her a few steps away from the gravesite.

A raindrop landed on top of her head. The clouds swirled, threatened. The sky opened up. Aimee turned to Tanner and leaned into him as more raindrops fell. She hadn't been honest about her cousin. BethAnne had been in love with someone for as long as Aimee could remember.

BethAnne had been hopelessly in love with Tanner.

3

Tanner whispered reassurances into Aimee's ear as she held onto him, as though clinging for dear life. He was still processing what had happened to one of his friends, and blocking out as much emotion as he could. BethAnne was one of the kindest people he'd ever known. They'd grown up together and been friends for what felt like forever. Losing her was hard enough. Losing her in this fashion made him want to put his fist through something, or someone. "We'll find the bastard responsible for this, and the person will pay."

Aimee responded with an almost imperceptible nod as rain came down in sheets, drenching them. His aunt would have told them to get out of the rain before they ended up catching their death from a cold. But Tanner knew a forklift couldn't move Aimee from this spot until her cousin was removed.

He couldn't be certain how long they stayed rooted to the same spot, relying on body heat to keep them warm. Photographs were taken from just about every angle before a team of EMTs arrived carrying a stretcher. He held Aimee tight against his chest, distracting her while BethAnne's body was removed from the now watery grave. The possibility, no matter how slight it might be, that he was responsible in any way for BethAnne's murder encased him in guilt.

This made him think of the other woman in his life who'd met with violence. His mother.

Don't even get him started on not being able to speak to her while she was in the hospital. She'd plead guilty to attempted murder and was beaten while on kitchen duty in jail awaiting trial. She was soon to be moved to a jail in Houston after the unprovoked attack, and was almost recovered enough for the transfer.

When did life get so complicated?

Another stab of guilt pierced his chest for not being grateful for being alive. BethAnne didn't get to have a complicated life anymore. She didn't get to have any kind of life anymore. She'd talked about having two kids one day, a boy and a girl. Tanner had rolled his eyes when BethAnne brought up hairbows and chubby-cheeked babies. Now? He wished she was around so he could take it back.

She hadn't mentioned dating anyone new lately. In fact, he was certain she wasn't dating at all, for reasons he couldn't figure out. BethAnne was outgoing and had no trouble striking up a conversation with strangers. She'd mentioned having a 'thing' for men in Wrangler jeans with cute backsides in a moment of 'too much information.' When he'd pointed out that he didn't have much of a point of comparison, not having spent too much time staring at cute male backsides, BethAnne had laughed to the point of snorting. Then, she'd teased him about not wanting a serious relationship. Ever. She'd said he should settle down one of these days. Have a couple of kids of his own. Again, he'd rolled his eyes at her.

The last time they'd been together was two weeks ago over margaritas and a cold beer at her favorite Tex-Mex spot north of Austin.

Hold on a second. There was someone. She'd talked about the possibility of a new guy in her life or, at the very least, hinted.

"Wasn't BethAnne involved with or crushing on a bull rider?" he whispered.

"Not to my knowledge," Aimee said. "She did like someone, though."

"I'm guessing she didn't say who it was, or you would have already supplied a name to the sheriff."

Aimee's body stiffened. Was this too much, too soon?

She took a step away and he immediately felt cold air where her body had been.

"What did she say to you?" she asked.

"It was more of a hint when I think about it," he supplied. "I teased her about spending a Saturday night with her friend when she could be out on a real date."

Aimee's eyebrow shot up. "What did she say to that?"

"She laughed and said she knew what she was getting with me. Said we'd have a great time, whereas she couldn't be so sure with someone she barely knew. I pressed her on the subject and she eventually mentioned a bull rider on the circuit might have caught her eye, but that he was on the road anyway, so it didn't matter."

"Then what happened?"

"She changed the subject," he admitted. "Turned the tables on me. Asked who I was interested in."

"And you said?"

"That I don't have time for any of that nonsense with a mother in jail and a family on the verge of falling apart," he explained.

"Is that true or just an excuse?" she asked.

He chuckled despite the heavy circumstances. "Probably both." Aimee was holding something back. He could see it in her eyes. Did it have something to do with her cousin?

"There might have been someone BethAnne had feelings for," Aimee said. "It's the only reason she would come hiking."

"What about going to her place to investigate before the sheriff gets a warrant or asks permission?" he asked, figuring there had to be some kind of clue at BethAnne's home in Lone Star Pass.

"As soon as they remove her from the premises, we can go," Aimee insisted.

Tanner held tight to Aimee as her cousin was lifted onto a stretcher. As hard as it was to look, he watched so Aimee wouldn't have to. She was placed on a stretcher that was then carried by a pair of muscular EMTs. Work on the ranch was hard but he couldn't fathom doing this. Of course, most of the time, this wasn't the case. EMTs saved lives, which had to be rewarding. There was a downside to every kind of work, and this had to be rock bottom for people who were trained to save others.

"You can turn around now," he said to Aimee as the EMTs reached the tree line. They would disappear soon.

Aimee reached for his hand, linking their fingers as soon as they made contact. As far as family members went, this had to be the most difficult thing to watch. He didn't envy her. Being a friend was enough of a gut punch.

Chin up, shoulders squared, Aimee watched as her cousin disappeared. He squeezed her hand to offer what little reassurance he could.

Physical contact with Aimee sent an electric current pulsing from the point of contact. Rather than get inside his head about what that meant—since it was a new feeling—he chalked it up to the extreme nature of their circumstances.

"Ready?" he asked when BethAnne could no longer be seen.

"Yes," Aimee relented.

"I need to swing by camp to gather up my tent. Okay?" He hoped it was because he wanted to stay together.

She nodded.

"How did you get here?" he asked.

"I drove."

"Okay," he said. "We can take my truck if you want. Or your vehicle. Or you can follow me."

"I'll follow you," she said. "I don't want to leave my car out here." A shiver caused her hand to tremble. She was cold despite wearing his jacket. They were drenched. The faster he got her out of here and to her cousin's apartment, where they could change clothes and warm up, the better as far as he was concerned.

A question remained. What had she been holding back earlier?

∽

IT WOULD BE impossible to shake off the overwhelming feeling of failure, so Aimee didn't try. She let the overwhelming feeling of failure envelop her.

There had to be something in her conversations with BethAnne that hinted something like this was possible. Because it was beyond her how her cousin could have been tricked into hiking, only to be murdered. BethAnne might not be the outdoorsy type, but that didn't mean she was completely incapable of taking care of herself. She'd grown up in this small town. She'd spent her summers outdoors like so many of her peers. It wasn't until the high school years that she'd traded in her boots for high heels and dirt on her face for shopping malls.

Aimee trailed behind Tanner, lost in thought as they made the short hike back to his tent. The winds had stripped trees of dead branches that now littered the landscape. The tent, however, stood strong. There was no doubt in her mind that Tanner was capable of surviving outdoors under extreme conditions. In fact, there was a lot of comfort in the thought.

While BethAnne had had a stable parents and upbringing, Aimee had been on the flighty branch of the family tree. She'd been saddled with a mother who'd just as soon run off with a guy than stick around to take care of her daughter. The opposite dynamic had always struck Aimee as odd. How could two families turn out so opposite? BethAnne and her mother had always been thick as thieves, as the saying went. Aimee had always admired their relationship.

BethAnne. What would Aimee do without her cousin now?

Back at the campsite, Tanner broke down the tent in a matter of minutes. It was an impressive feat when she really thought about it. The other impressive thing about Tanner was his self-sufficiency. The man was an island and made no secret about preferring it that way. It made sense from everything she knew about ranchers. They spent more time than most people realized mending fences and alone on the land. Another big part of their time was spent on paperwork. They had to monitor and report every aspect of their herd, individually. Ranching, she'd learned, was more about paperwork than expected. The rest of the time was spent outdoors.

BethAnne had always been quick to provide updates on Tanner. His ability to track dangerous poachers was the stuff of legend. *BethAnne.*

Aimee could scarcely imagine never having another conversation with her cousin. Never having another margarita. Never going on another girls' trip to Galveston to visit the Strand or the Pier.

Reality hit hard, punching a hole in the center of her chest.

"Let's head down," Tanner said, breaking through her revelry as she stood there, freezing. The wind had picked up but the rain had calmed down at least a little bit.

For now, anyway.

"Okay," she said. It was strange leaving this place without BethAnne. Aimee had convinced herself they would find BethAnne alive, covered in poison ivy or something silly like that. If only.

The trip down was quiet and Aimee realized Tanner must be hurting as much as she was. They'd both hoped… prayed…to find her cousin alive. It was the reason they'd planned to wait out the storm so they could keep searching. Neither had allowed themselves to consider this as a possible outcome.

Tanner tossed his supplies into the backseat of the dual cab pickup truck he drove, with the Firebrand Ranch logo on the back windshield. She'd heard about the Firebrands and all the money they had. She'd heard about their social position. She remembered the fact Tanner didn't give her a second glance all those years ago before BethAnne insisted she come to Austin for visits instead of the other way around. The visits to Lone Star Pass had stopped and Aimee didn't see Tanner again, until now, until years later.

Tanner represented honor and chivalry, which was not

lost on her. In fact, she welcomed someone opening car doors for her and treating her like she was special. There were far too few occasions in life where she'd been treated like she belonged, let alone pampered.

In the truck, Tanner started the engine and turned to her. "Was there something you were holding back up there about BethAnne?"

"What do you mean?"

"I don't know," he started. "I got the feeling there was something you wanted to say but stopped yourself when we were talking about liking someone."

"Oh, that," she said.

He waited, tapping his thumb on the wheel. "Because I thought there might be someone she liked too. But she would never name the guy. Maybe we'll figure it out once we get to her place."

For a split-second, Aimee considered telling him the person BethAnne had liked was him. But what good would it do now? Her cousin would have been embarrassed for him to find out this way. Rather than bark up that tree, Aimee decided to give her cousin what dignity she could.

"I'm sure we will," Aimee said, thinking she would go to her own grave with that secret. "Right now, I'm just happy to have heat." She rubbed her hands together in front of the vent to warm them faster.

Tanner smiled. She hadn't seen that a whole lot in their time together, which was no surprise under the circumstances, only now she realized that he had one of those smiles that lit campfires inside her. This man had a dangerous effect on her. It would be so easy to lean into him, into the comfort he offered in his strong arms and calm demeanor. There was a steadiness about him that drew her like a magnet to steel.

It was easy to see why her cousin had fallen for him.

The rest of the ride over to BethAnne's was spent in companionable silence. Tanner pulled up in front of the two-bedroom bungalow. She'd been renting the place for two years before the owner said she could buy it outright. BethAnne had been thrilled. The closing would have been next Friday.

With no siblings, Aimee would have to go through her cousin's personal affairs and set things straight. Her aunt wouldn't have the stomach for it. Aimee would have to be the one to do it, to go through BethAnne's belongings. Aimee made a mental note to double-check with her aunt, on the off chance she wanted to be part of the process.

"I need to be there when they inform my aunt and uncle of what happened," she reminded Tanner.

"Did Lawler give you any indication of when that might be?"

The sheriff could be heading over there right now for all she knew. "I should probably reach out to Lawler to find out what his plans are."

"I highly doubt he'll want to wait," Tanner said. "Families deserve to know, and he won't want them to find out from someone other than him."

"True," she agreed. "I don't see any reason for him to hold off."

"BethAnne was close with her mother," he said wistfully.

"Yes, she was," Aimee concurred. It was strange to refer to her cousin in the past tense. In fact, everything seemed so surreal, like she was trapped in an alternate universe. "It's so hard to believe this is happening."

"I know," Tanner agreed with warmth and compassion in his voice.

There was a note in his voice that drew her in, made her want to scoot closer to him just to be in his warmth.

As strong as the pull toward this man was, Aimee could never allow anything to happen between them. It wouldn't be right.

So, she would fight her feelings toward Tanner Firebrand. And, just like in the past when they were young, and he was her 'older guy' crush, she would win. She had to.

4

The drive to BethAnne's bungalow took a little more than an hour without traffic. Tanner talked Aimee into allowing him to have her vehicle towed so they could ride together. Her sedan would arrive shortly after they did, according to the driver. They stopped off for food at one of those new mega stop stations that dotted Texas highways. The place had everything from made-to-order sandwiches and barbeque plates to their own special beef jerky. They'd picked up and eaten a pair of brisket sandwiches that he hoped he wouldn't regret later.

The ride was mostly quiet as Aimee leaned back in the seat and kept her eyes closed for most of it. Said she didn't sleep, but it was enough to power down. Said she wanted to be ready to go once they got to BethAnne's place.

The downtown bungalow off Main Street was dark. Winds had let up and the rain had stopped, but clouds still blanketed the sky. He still tried to shake off the image of BethAnne in that shallow grave, and failed miserably. Which meant he needed to get to work trying to figure out who would do such a horrific thing to another human being, let alone someone as kind as BethAnne.

As he parked on the parking pad beside the bungalow, Aimee sat straight up with a disoriented look on her face.

"Are we here?" she asked, rubbing her eyes and looking around. Her voice sounded like she was in a fog. Had she dosed off?

"We made it," he said. He cut off the engine, exited the vehicle, and then headed around the front to open her door. "Your car will be here soon." He checked his cell. "In fact, the driver just reported that he's fifteen minutes out."

"It'll give us a few minutes to look around," she said on a yawn as she climbed down and out of the truck, and then stretched out her arms.

"Do you have an overnight bag in your car?" he asked, watching as she dug around in her purse for a key to the front door.

"I don't need one when I come here to see BethAnne," she supplied. "I have a couple of drawers in her guest room filled with everything I need."

Tanner always kept a ready-bag in his truck, so he pulled out the rucksack. Aimee shot a look his way that would have made him crack a smile under normal circumstances. Was she jealous?

Since losing BethAnne, nothing was funny. He kept an overnight bag packed in his truck at all times because of poachers, not hook-ups. He could be called out at various times during the night or day for an emergency with the cattle that could lead to him spending the night out on the property with little to no notice. It was just easier to keep extra supplies on hand.

He shouldered the rucksack that was a whole separate deal from his camping supplies, and then followed Aimee inside the house. Walking into BethAnne's house without her here put a strange feeling in the pit of his stomach. He'd stopped by on occasion to pick her up, although they normally met up, taking separate vehicles when they went out for drinks.

"I can use a quick shower and a strong cup of coffee," he said to Aimee.

"I'd like to burn my clothing," she said with a nod of agreement. "Is it weird that I never want to see this outfit again, let alone wear it?"

"No, it's not," he said. "And I couldn't agree more." Hell, he'd burn everything he had on to avoid seeing the clothes he'd been wearing when his friend was found dead. He'd like to erase everything about this day, this memory, except that wouldn't help find the person responsible for the murder. "The sheriff didn't say this was a possibility, but it should be easy enough to search online to see if there have been any other similar murders."

"It was a distinct way of killing her, wasn't it?"

"What is your first thought about the method?" he asked. Then, thought better of it. "Hold that thought." He needed a shower and coffee for this discussion. "Give me ten minutes."

"Same," she said.

He held up a finger before retrieving a trash bag from the kitchen. "Use this for your clothes. I'll do away with yours and mine too, so we never have to look at them again."

"I'll set it outside the bathroom door when I'm done," she said. "I'll use BethAnne's bathroom so you can use the guest one."

He handed over the bag with a nod of approval. Aimee disappeared down the hallway to BethAnne's room after making a pit stop in the guest room to grab fresh clothes. He picked up his rucksack and made the trek down the hall to what would be his bathroom.

The door opened and closed twice in the master, so he figured it was safe to grab the trash bag. It sat on the outside of the door, as promised. He picked it up and took it into the guest bath with him before stripping down. He threw the pile in the bag along with the shoes he'd been wearing. Aimee had done the same. Then, he wrapped a towel around his waist and took the clothes to the brown bin right outside the back door before heading back inside and locking the door behind him. Last year, he wouldn't have remembered to lock a door while in Lone Star Pass, but there'd been crimes aimed at the general public, and at his loved ones over the last year, and now it had become habit.

Shame, he thought. Part of the benefits of living in a small town was not ever having to lock a door or worry about crime. He was learning the hard way; the only constant was change. In fact, stand in one spot long enough, and everything would look different given enough time.

Tanner took a quick shower, careful to scrub every inch of skin.

By the time he dressed and returned to the small kitchen, he could hear that Aimee was finishing up in the master. He put on a pot of coffee. A few minutes later, he had a full, warm cup in his hand. The brisket sat on his stomach, but he figured that had more to do with the stress of the day than the quality of the food. Surprisingly, the gas station/mega mart had had decent offerings.

"Mind if I pour a cup?" Aimee asked, joining him in the small kitchen.

He picked up the mug on the counter. "It's ready. All you have to do is fix it up however you like it."

"Black is good," she said, taking the offering and rubbing

the mug around in her palms. She blew on the top before taking a sip. Then, she locked gazes with him. "The obvious reason someone would sew another person's mouth closed right before or after they took their life, would be to make a statement about shutting them up."

Tanner nodded, his heart heavy at hearing the words from her that he'd heard inside his own thoughts. He located his cell and pulled up an internet surfing app from the home screen. He set his coffee down and typed in a few key words. Waited.

Nothing came up.

"Doesn't mean murders like this aren't happening," he pointed out as they stared at the screen.

"Just means they might not be reported yet," she said.

"That's right. Plus, some counties might not be releasing details of other murders to the public, since this is such a heinous act," he confirmed.

"Why would they do that? Why would the law keep information from citizens? Wouldn't that put more women at risk?"

"Doing so could run a risk of creating copycat killers or ending up with a host of unwanted tips that could flood their system." He picked his coffee up and took a sip. "That's off the top of my head. It doesn't mean they aren't working together behind the scenes, though."

Aimee drummed her fingers on the counter. She'd changed into a white mock turtle neck and sweatpants. Her hair was still soaked. Beads of water dripped onto her shirt. He shouldn't notice any of these things under the circumstances. But he did. And just as quickly, he shifted his focus back to the case. "Without interviewing anyone, we don't know if someone was mad at her or holding a grudge."

"There were fertility cases that got heated when pregnancies didn't happen sometimes," Aimee recalled.

"I heard about a few of those. No names, though. Beth-Anne wouldn't violate privacy laws with details that could identify her patients," he explained.

Aimee tapped her finger on the side of her mug. Her gaze unfocused like she'd gone to another place mentally. "It's strange being here without her, knowing she won't walk through that door again."

Tanner couldn't agree more.

∼

"It's the worst," Tanner said as Aimee took a tentative step toward him. She debated her actions for a half second until he locked gazes with her and all logic flew out the window. The air immediately changed in the room as electricity pinged between them. The air charged as she reached for him.

"Hold me?" she asked, surprised when he immediately hauled her against his chest and wrapped her in an embrace. Her body melted into his.

"Kiss me?"

"Yes," he said as she raised her face to him. The second their eyes met, she knew she was in deep trouble.

Aimee's breath caught in her throat the second Tanner's lips touched hers. It was as though a bomb detonated in the center of her chest, and warmth pulsed from it to all her uniquely feminine places. This close, she breathed in his clean, spicy male scent. Thick black lashes hooded the most incredible pair of golden-brown eyes.

She closed hers to lessen some of the physical impact he was having on her, not that it did a whole lot of good. Her body sprung to life as he teased her mouth open with his tongue. The tip darted inside, causing another one of those sensual bombs to detonate. Goosebumps raised on her arms and a wave of desire washed over her and through her. The way he moved his tongue inside her mouth sent need spiraling through her. This man was perfection as his hands, rough from a hard day of labor, roamed over her shoulders, caressing her. More of that warmth pooled between the sensitive skin of her inner thighs.

Aimee parted her lips as he drove his tongue inside. She matched him stroke for stroke as her pulse raced and breathing became more difficult.

Remembering that BethAnne had wanted to be with this man more than she wanted air, was the equivalent of a bucket of ice water poured over Aimee's head. She took a step back, brought the back of her hand up to her mouth, and then tried to catch her breath. Locking gazes would be too risky a move while she was still in the haze that was Tanner's lips. She could only imagine what else they could do, considering how worked up she was now. Her heart thundered inside her chest, hammering the inside of her ribcage.

There was something about the tenderness with which he started the kiss, full of sensual promise, that had robbed her ability to breathe the moment their lips touched. If he was this good at kissing, she could only imagine what sex would be like.

She stopped herself right there. "That can't happen again."

"Agreed," he said. The fact his response had been almost immediate caused her heart to sink. She had good reasons why they couldn't kiss again. A solid excuse. For him, was it a preference? Did he not like kissing her? Was she bad at it?

Aimee shuttered those thoughts. Something in his eyes told her that he was into her, no matter what his words said. Eyes didn't lie and his had been filled with appreciation and desire. Still, she didn't have it in her heart to ask him the real reason. Facing rejection right now wasn't high on her list. Besides, her emotions were all over the place and his probably were too. It was most likely the reason she'd asked for the kiss in the first place. Right now, though, she needed a distraction. The small sandwich she'd had on the road sat hard in her stomach. She needed something else to fill it. "Do you think you can eat?"

"We probably should," he said, looking just as disoriented as her about the turn of events.

"I'll fix something." She moved to the fridge and opened it. BethAnne loved to eat and she was a good cook so there should be plenty to work with in the kitchen. "How about breakfast tacos?"

"What can I do to help?" he asked.

"Pour another round of coffee." She pulled out ingredients and set them on the counter next to the stove. The bacon could be microwaved. The eggs scrambled with a light dusting of cheddar cheese. Then, all she had left to do was set out the sour cream, salsa, and mix up some guacamole. The latter would take the longest, so she took care of making it first. Two avocados would be plenty, along with lime, salt, red onion, and Roma tomatoes. For the rest, she cut up fresh cilantro and minced garlic.

There was something calming about the routine of cooking. Being in BethAnne's kitchen brought back a flood of good memories of the two of them cooking in here. Some of BethAnne's favorites were homemade pizza baked on a cooking stone and fajitas. Her cousin made the best margaritas, even though she preferred to go out for them.

The memories made her smile. A wave of guilt followed for kissing Tanner. What would her cousin have said if she'd known about the kiss? The last thing Aimee would ever want to do was hurt her cousin.

A voice in the back of her mind pointed out that was impossible to do now, thanks to a bastard who deserved to pay the price. BethAnne deserved justice.

"Here you go." Tanner's voice broke into her heavy thoughts. He set down a fresh cup of coffee next to her on the counter. His body was so close she could feel his warmth.

"Thank you," she said after clearing her throat. It was a little too easy to get caught up in all that was Tanner Firebrand. After taking a sip, she went back to work scrambling eggs and microwave-cooking the bacon. Street taco tortillas worked the best, so she pulled those out and heated them up on the flame of the gas stove before piling on the eggs and bacon pieces. All that was left to do was add guac, sour cream, and salsa, which she let Tanner do for himself. Getting the perfect combination of flavors was different for everyone.

Tanner thanked her before taking his plate over to the dining room table. It had six chairs and was a focal point between the living room and kitchen. BethAnne loved to entertain, and dinners were a big part of that. She had coworkers over. She had a few neighbors over, speaking of whom, Aimee figured they should make the rounds with them to see if anyone saw a new person hanging around. A benefit of living in a small town, BethAnne had often remarked, was having neighbors who looked out for each other. Maybe someone had seen a new person coming and going. It was worth a shot.

Aimee joined Tanner after cutting off the flame. "I was

just thinking we should ask around to see if anyone saw a new person coming in and out of the house."

"As much as BethAnne entertained, we might be chasing our tails, but I'm game to try anything at this point." Tanner took a bite and then chewed. "This is amazing, by the way."

She smiled a genuine smile at the compliment. "It can't hurt to try. I was thinking we could start with the neighbors, since we're already here."

"Good idea. I'm wondering if we can call her cell phone provider to ask about texts or phone calls within the last couple of days."

"The sheriff will be working that angle too," she said. "Phone providers are picky about privacy, but we can try."

He nodded. "When do you want to swing by her workplace?"

"I was thinking that we start with looking around here at the house before canvassing the neighbors. Then, work our way to the office," she said. "How does that sound?"

"Like a solid start," he said. "I'm sorry about the kiss before. I was out of line."

He was out of line?

"Last time I checked, I was the one who asked you to kiss me," she said, feeling heat crawl up her neck.

"Still," he said. "I apologize for overstepping my bounds."

Why did he feel the need to say he was sorry for a kiss that he didn't even ask for? Was it part of his cowboy code?

Or was he embarrassed?

5

Tanner pulled his act together. Aimee was upset and she wanted a sense of normalcy. It was the only reason she'd asked for the kiss in the first place. He didn't want to be anyone's momentary comfort, least of all hers. He'd gone down that road before with someone else and it had ended badly. He'd been all but directly accused of taking advantage of an emotional situation. Aubrey Diamond, of Diamond J Cattle, had been going through a divorce. He'd genuinely felt sorry for her. After a few too many glasses of wine, she'd come onto him like nobody's business. The right thing to do would have been to walk away. She'd begged him not to and then decided not to take no for an answer.

The fact he'd been attracted to her for years, even though she'd been with someone else, weighed in on his decision to 'go with the flow' as she'd put it. She'd asked him to stop fighting their feelings. He'd been honest and upfront that, yes, he was attracted to her, but no, he didn't want anything serious.

Aubrey had jumped on the chance to date, promising

the last thing she wanted was a committed relationship after a divorce. He'd believed her. A month in, things got messy between them. Aubrey became possessive and said she'd changed her mind about having a real relationship. Told him that she was falling for him. He wasn't seeing anyone else because he believed in monogamy, but he reminded her of their conversation so as not to create expectations that would ultimately let her down. He'd believed her once again when she said she could live with that as long as he didn't date anyone else while they were together. He promised that he wouldn't but said he wasn't the commitment type for the long haul.

Things became more and more complicated between them when she wanted to leave a bag over at his place to make sleepovers more convenient. Tanner didn't do overnight bags or girlfriends. His refusal caused more friction.

Then came the public displays of affection, which was another thing he couldn't stand. If he was dating someone, he didn't mind holding hands, putting his arm around his lady, or the occasional kiss. Mugging down in a public place or groping when others were around were deal breakers for him.

Boy, did Aubrey not appreciate him telling her that he needed space. At first, she cried. Then, she got mad. After that, she started popping onto the ranch to see him out of the blue, which he later realized was her way of checking up on him.

And then, she went around town talking about how she had to break it off with him because he'd become too clingy. He'd watched his older brother Kellan go through a divorce that had wrecked him, so he had some knowledge of what they did to a person's mental state. Aubrey, however, had gone off the rails with demands.

When he finally cut her loose, she stayed mad and started rumors about him. Unfortunately, with his side of the family's reputation, some folks believed her, and he got side-eye at the grocery store from some of her friends as well as people he'd known since the third grade. Seemed like the whole town took her side and automatically believed he was the bad guy, so he wasn't about to touch that hot stove twice.

Not that he believed Aimee was the type of person who would do something like that. His gut instinct said she was a good person. Honest. But her emotions were extreme right now and it didn't feel right to take advantage even if that wasn't his intention in the first place. It hadn't been with Aubrey either and look how that had turned out.

"You cooked, which means I do dishes," he said as he stood up from the table. She opened her mouth to argue but then clamped it shut. "That way, you can start looking around in BethAnne's personal belongings, to see if you find anything to work with."

"Okay," she said as she stood up and then walked over to the sink to rinse off her plate. She set her coffee mug in and then turned around. "I was thinking that I'd start with her laptop, even though I don't know her password. I can make a guess and then call her cell provider to see if they'll give me access. The sheriff asked me not to interfere with his investigation, but I don't see how that would qualify. We should be alright asking the neighbors questions too. Visiting her job starts getting tricky, but BethAnne is...*was*...my cousin and I can say that I've stopped by to pick up her personal effects. I don't see how the sheriff could get riled up over that."

"BethAnne's personal effects at work might be pushing

it." Tanner hated to be a buzzkill. He didn't want to see Aimee get into trouble while digging around. "I'd hate to cross a line there. Neighbors are fair game and so is talking to folks at work. Taking anything that might be considered evidence could start pushing the boundary."

Aimee pursed her lips. "Those are good points. I'd like to speak to the doctor to see if any patients or co-workers had a problem with BethAnne."

"I'll double-check the news to see if any information has gotten out about the murder or the way in which BethAnne was..."

He couldn't bring himself to finish his sentence. Losing BethAnne was going to be hard no matter what happened. "Anyway, if folks around the neighborhood know, they might be on high alert. Same with her work folks. I'd rather get a natural reaction from them if that makes sense."

"It does," she said as he loaded the dishwasher. The task didn't take long considering there was only two of them, and she'd cleaned as she went while chopping and cooking. "Getting a pure reaction will be good. Imaginations can run wild once they know what happened."

Aimee's cell buzzed. She retrieved it and checked the screen. "I don't recognize the number. Should I answer?"

"I would," he urged.

Aimee nodded and hit the green 'button' on the screen before putting the call on speaker. "Hello?"

"Aimee Anderson, this is Sheriff Lawler."

"Hello, Sheriff."

"I'm calling because the coroner has had a chance to finish an initial examination on the victim and I thought you deserved to know his thoughts," Sheriff Lawler said.

"I'd like that very much, Sheriff."

"I need to warn you that what I'm about to say is graphic," he continued. "You might want to sit down."

"I'm good, but thank you for the warning," she said.

"Alright then. I'll get right to it. The victim died by asphyxiation due to being strangled with a rope, equivalent to the kind used for roping horses and calving in competitions," Sheriff Lawler explained. "I'd appreciate your discretion with this information since it won't be released publicly at this time."

"I'll keep it to myself," she promised.

"Rope fibers were also found in Ms. Dyer's clothing. I'm sending those off to the lab to be analyzed, but please don't expect an answer in an hour or even a couple of days. I know this isn't something you want to hear, but real investigations take time. It's not like on TV where every question has an answer in a matter of hours and the whole case is wrapped up neatly in an hour episode."

"Didn't believe it was," Aimee said after taking in a slow breath. Tanner's heart ached for her upon hearing this news. As good of friends as he'd been with BethAnne, it wasn't the same thing as growing up together as cousins. He had nine in his family and had grown up close to a couple of them. So, he couldn't imagine how much worse this news was for her. On the surface, she was holding it together well. The determination and laser focus in her expression right now was probably the main things holding her together. And damned if he didn't want to hold her, kiss her, take care of her until she could sleep at night again, despite the fact she didn't need those things to survive. No, Aimee was strong and a survivor. She'd shared a little bit about her past. Someone like her had a story.

The walls she'd erected around her heart had come back

up the minute he apologized for the kiss, which he now regretted. Not the kiss, but the apology.

Not that any of it mattered.

He refused to take advantage of someone in a vulnerable position again. She might not realize how susceptible she was right now. And he'd be damned before he would put her in a position to resent him in any way. Once the investigation was behind them, he hoped the two of them could stay in touch. Maybe even become friends?

Bad idea, Firebrand. Friendship wasn't exactly what his heart wanted.

Thankfully, he was mature enough to infuse logic into the situation instead of running off half-cocked with his heart leading the way.

And he intended to keep it that way.

∽

Fire raged through Aimee at the sheriff's revelation. She wanted to know the details of what happened to BethAnne and she didn't want to know. Needed to know was more like it. "Will the coroner perform a complete autopsy on my cousin to find out if she was…"

She couldn't bring herself to say the word *raped*.

"Yes," Sheriff Lawler confirmed. "There will be a complete workup. Once again, it takes time." Meanwhile the bastard who did this to BethAnne was out on the loose, running around and able to do this to another human being. Aimee couldn't stand the fact another family might have to go through something like this, as another life was snuffed out senselessly.

"Have you notified my aunt and uncle?"

"Yes, ma'am," the sheriff confirmed. "I delivered the news personally."

Her cell buzzed in her hand. "This must be one of them calling to tell me." Of course, she needed to talk to them to see if they were okay after hearing this horrific news and chided herself for not being there when the sheriff informed them of the fact their beloved daughter had been murdered. "How much detail did you go into with them?"

"Not as much as I have with you, to be honest." The sheriff's radio squawked. "You were onsite. You saw what happened. They're on the way down to my office where I'll give them more information about the murder and also ask them to keep the details quiet while we investigate. I'd also like to keep the particulars of this out of the news media for as long as possible, because folks have a tendency to come out of the woodwork and complicate things."

"Does this mean you believe the crime is personal?" she asked.

"At this time, I'd rather not comment on anything but facts," he said. A note in his voice made her believe he was holding information back. At this point, he had to have at least a few suspects in mind other than Alicia.

The cell stopped buzzing, indicating the call went to voicemail. "Thank you for the information, Sheriff. I'd better call my relatives back before they worry about me."

"You're welcome, Ms. Anderson."

Aimee ended the call and then immediately checked her recent calls. Sure enough, her aunt showed as a missed call. A notification hadn't popped up for voicemail yet, but her aunt was notorious for leaving long messages so that wasn't surprising since she'd barely missed the call. After taking in a slow, deep breath, Aimee tapped the name and waited for her aunt to pick up. It only took one ring.

Her aunt sobbed into the line, her pain palpable even through a cell. "Aimee, I have bad news about our sweet…"

"I know, Aunt Denise," Aimee confirmed with as reassuring a voice as possible. "I was there searching with everyone when she was…I'm so sorry about BethAnne."

"Of course, you were. My mind isn't right." Aunt Denise paused. "Someone hurt my baby." She'd always been a fierce protector of BethAnne, who was an only child, same as Aimee. They'd been close enough to consider themselves sisters, which is what they told people most of the time anyway. They might not look too much alike, but there was a family resemblance between them if someone paid attention.

"I know, Aunt Denise," Aimee soothed. "I'm so sorry."

"They hurt her real bad," Aunt Denise said before another couple of sobs came through that nearly cracked Aimee's heart in half. She'd taken the call off speaker and was now walking toward the back door to get some privacy and air.

"It's not fair," she consoled, wishing there were magic words to make this feel better and knowing she would fall woefully short in any attempts to make this alright. It would never be alright again. Period. BethAnne was gone and she had to figure out a way to live without her best friend.

"Who would do something like this?" Aunt Denise continued. "The sheriff said my baby was…murdered." She sobbed out the last word.

"I don't have the first clue, Aunt Denise." Aimee wished she had a trail to follow. "I can't believe she's gone." A few rogue tears spilled down Aimee's cheeks. She was so not a crier. In fact, she was known for holding everything in. BethAnne, on the other hand, wore her emotions on her sleeve. She'd had a big personality. She'd loved big. She'd had big dreams. "But I promise not to rest until we figure out who did this to her and why."

Aunt Denise broke down on the line. The sniffles ripped Aimee's heart to shreds. "I'm sorry." She managed to get the words out through sobs.

"Don't be, Aunt Denise." Aimee could scarcely bear to hear her aunt this way. "BethAnne didn't deserve to have this happen to her. She was one of the kindest, most genuine people who ever walked this earth. Only a monster would touch a hair on her head." Aimee didn't look forward to the moment when her aunt learned just how heinous the crime against BethAnne had been. Even after having a few hours to process the crime scene, Aimee still couldn't believe her best friend was dead, let alone how it had happened.

The sheriff wasn't exactly trading ideas on who could have done this. She couldn't help but wonder how much progress he'd made on the investigation that he wasn't sharing.

"I can't believe this is real," Aunt Denise said.

"Neither can I," Aimee confirmed. "How is Uncle Chuckie?"

"Not good," Aunt Denise said. "He grabbed his shotgun and threw it in the backseat. I don't know what he thinks he's going to do with it, considering the sheriff would lock him up for walking around in public threatening the first man he came across."

"I'm sure Uncle Chuckie will calm down." Aimee figured the man would be seeing red right now. "It'll be good for him to speak to the sheriff and maybe get a minute to bring his anger back down to a reasonable level." Uncle Chuckie had always been protective of his only daughter. He'd believed BethAnne hung the moon. "Please tell him that I love him and we'll get through this somehow. I don't know how just yet, but we will. And we'll find the bastard who did this to BethAnne. He won't get away with it."

Now, Aimee was reduced to tears.

In a surprise move, Tanner came up behind her and looped his arms around her waist. She leaned into him, back to chest, and absorbed just a little bit of his strength.

It would be a mistake to get too used to this. But for right now, she didn't have the strength to fight what she wanted…him.

6

As much discord and fighting as there had been in Tanner's family, he couldn't fathom having a conversation like the one Aimee was having with her aunt. It broke his heart. All he wanted to do was find a way to offer some small comfort.

Holding her was all he could think to do while she finished the call.

"Call me whenever you need to talk, Aunt Denise." After a few uh-huhs and an *I love you*, Aimee ended the call. She didn't turn around right away. Instead, she stood there, staring at nothing in particular and, he figured, trying to pull it together.

He couldn't be certain how many minutes ticked by. Didn't care either. The only thing that mattered to him was Aimee.

"I should probably look around to see what I can find," she finally said after clearing her throat. She sniffed a few times and then straightened her shoulders, like he realized she always did when she was gathering herself.

"Where do you want me to start?" he asked as he

followed her back inside.

When she turned around to face him, he stared into red-rimmed eyes. "Maybe the kitchen?"

"I'll check drawers," he said. "If I remember correctly, BethAnne used to keep a mishmash of papers in one of them."

Aimee pointed. "Top righthand drawer over there."

Drawing on his willpower, he walked away from her to rifle through the pantry. There was something wrong about going through someone's personal effects without them in the room, and yet it had to be done. Better him than a stranger.

"I'll check out the master bedroom," Aimee said. "Beth-Anne kept personal things in her bedside drawer and her laptop was always within arm's reach."

She disappeared down the hall. The wood flooring creaked with her footsteps. It would be impossible to sneak up on someone in this house.

Was that the reason the bastard lured BethAnne away from home to kill her? The stitching on her mouth made him think there was no way this was random. She couldn't have decided to go hiking—again, something she normally wouldn't be caught dead doing—and then a person she'd never met before killing her in such a personal way. First of all, she'd been strangled. BethAnne was one of the most paranoid people he'd ever met. It wasn't likely someone would be able to surprise her from behind. She was always watching over her shoulder. The weather had been spotty over the past few days. Strong winds could have masked other noises.

The bigger question was why she'd driven to the hiking trail in the first place And why there? If she'd wanted to take a walk, wouldn't she have made a loop around the block or gone down the street to the park? Why get in her car and drive somewhere when she could get exercise right here?

A phone call?

The sheriff wasn't exactly sharing all the information. Aimee had planned to call the phone company before the sheriff's phone call interrupted her thoughts. He imagined that would come after checking around the house for papers. All he was finding in the drawer so far was tax receipts and paid bills.

The floor creaked. Aimee was coming.

The minute she walked into the room, he knew she'd found something serious. Aimee scraped her top teeth over her bottom lip. She held out a yellow piece of paper for him to see.

"Someone is pregnant."

"BethAnne?"

"No," Aimee said immediately. "We were best friends. She would have told me before now."

"Why would she have a positive pregnancy test from work, here at home?" he asked. It didn't make sense to hide, especially when there was no name on the paperwork. Which was puzzling. "Don't doctor offices always write the name of the patient on the header?"

"Usually, yes," she confirmed. "That's part of the reason this caught me off guard. The top is always filled out. One of the sheets goes to billing. The other generally is handed to the patient."

"If she was hiding a pregnancy, someone might have killed her to keep their secret," he surmised, hoping that wasn't the case.

"I was just thinking the same thing," she confirmed with a frown that caused his chest to squeeze in pain.

"An affair might be a good reason for someone to want

to hide a pregnancy," he continued.

"The stitches would make more sense that way," she said, grimacing.

"Except, why kill her and then stitch her mouth together?" He started pacing in the small kitchen.

"Good question," she said.

He snapped his fingers as a logical answer came to him. "It's a threat to anyone else who might know the secret."

"There are only a handful of reasons to hide a pregnancy," Aimee piggybacked onto his thought.

"An affair was already mentioned," he said. "Another reason might be an abusive boyfriend or husband."

"She might have been hiding the pregnancy for a friend who was in trouble," Aimee agreed. "It sounds like something BethAnne would do."

"My mind snaps back to fertility issues," he said. "What if someone went to a sperm bank and didn't want their spouse to find out?"

"It's reasonable to me, except what is the threat about?" she asked. "Why not just kill BethAnne if that's the case? Why sew her mouth shut?"

"That's the real question, isn't it," he said. At least they were starting to make some sense out of a senseless act.

"BethAnne might have been threatening to tell the father," she said. "It makes sense if you think about it. Others might know or be involved in hiding the pregnancy, but BethAnne knew the father too and didn't think it was right to keep him in the dark."

Now, Aimee was pacing too.

"Which rules out an abusive relationship because BethAnne would never throw another human being under the bus."

"You're right," Aimee agreed. "She definitely wouldn't.

She would put herself in harm's way to protect someone else."

"I like the hidden pregnancy angle," he said, realizing how that sounded and wishing he could reel the words in to say it better. "With the threat, it also means someone else knew. Someone is sitting on a secret."

"More than one person," she corrected. "Because the pregnant person is also in on it and most likely the one behind all the secrecy."

"So, she believed she was protecting someone," he said. "And possibly got wrapped up in a bad situation, which cost her life. Someone decided to use her as a threat to others, a cautionary tale."

"Makes more sense than the serial killer scenario, given the circumstances," she said. "Someone asked her to meet them for a hike. She might not have thought anything about it, which is why she texted me that she was hiking. It wasn't her normal thing, so she was clearly being lured out there."

"She texted you but didn't think anything about it," he pointed out. "Which likely meant that she trusted the person."

"And they might have asked her not to tell anyone they were meeting." Aimee issued a sharp sigh. "I think we might find answers at her workplace."

Could they waltz in and start asking questions without raising any eyebrows, or worse, getting turned in to the sheriff?

∾

"Let's head out to Dr. Carrol's office now," Tanner said to Aimee. "We know the sheriff is waiting for your aunt and uncle, so we won't run into him."

"I feel like I should stop by there and see them. Maybe on the way back from the doctor's office?" Aimee was not looking forward to seeing her aunt break down in person. It had been bad enough to hear the sobs over the phone. Even so, she wanted to give the woman a hug and, truth be known, Aimee could use one from her aunt too.

"That's doable," he confirmed.

"And I think we should at least talk to Mrs. Weller across the street before we head out," she said. "I know she keeps her finger on the pulse of what's going on in the neighborhood. She'll be a good resource, and she's always home according to BethAnne. Mrs. Weller is a widow who runs a business from home."

"Good. Sounds like she'll be there. We can swing by right now," Tanner said. He'd been nothing but helpful and kind. Should she tell him how her cousin truly felt about him? A piece of her believed he should know the truth since BethAnne had never been able to tell him. Aimee still felt guilty for asking him to kiss her.

Again, the voice in the back of her mind reminded her that BethAnne was gone and she wasn't coming back. The sheriff's words were starting to sink in. "Who did my cousin know from the rodeo circuit, by the way?"

"The rope?" he asked. "That would be common in these parts. We use it at the ranch."

Would that make him a suspect? Aimee hadn't thought about it before, because she knew that he'd been just as shocked as her at seeing the body. He'd been one of the first to volunteer for the search too. Bottom line, he cared a great deal about BethAnne.

"I thought about that too," he said as he studied her. It probably wasn't difficult to guess what she was thinking.

"What?" she asked, just to confirm.

"The fact I could end up a suspect in this case," he said. "The sheriff has been treating me like a witness so far, but that could change in a heartbeat. I'm well aware of the fact." The look of disdain on his face was another reason she believed him. No one was good enough of an actor to fake that look. He was genuine.

"He better not," was all she said. "Besides, between the law and the two of us, we'll figure out who is responsible. And this is ranching country. Like you said, everyone uses this same kind of rope. That would make almost one hundred percent of the town suspect."

"I don't know if you paid attention at the site, but Beth-Anne was dragged at least partially to the grave," he said. "Plus, someone had to dig it in the first place. If this was premeditated, they could have done it in advance."

"What are you getting at?"

"The fact Sheriff Lawler can probably rule out most women in the county, which narrows the list down quite a bit," he explained.

"Unless more than one person was involved," she stated. "Two women could drag a person."

"Maybe," he said. "But did you see the sheriff looking at tracks?"

She shook her head. In the heat of the moment, all she could recall—and this was barely—was the shallow grave and the absent look on her cousin's face. The lack of vitality. The stitches would haunt her dreams. Other than the nap in the truck, Aimee had no plans to sleep for a long time. Not until the bastard who did this was brought to justice.

"There was only one set and the footprint was large," he said. "It looked like a man's shoe."

"There's no chance someone is being framed, right?"

"I guess we won't know that until we get a name," he reasoned.

"Let's go across the street and see what Mrs. Weller has to say," she said, rubbing her arms to warm them. Suddenly, they felt cold. She was still trying to process what had happened and the fact BethAnne was dead. Her cousin had always been so animated, so lively. Seeing her in the grave didn't seem real. It was like a nightmare that she hoped to wake up from any moment to find a very angry BethAnne. Angry because Aimee and Tanner had kissed, in her kitchen no less. Angry that Aimee and Tanner had teamed up. And angry that Aimee and Tanner were going through her drawers and personal things.

Another rogue tear escaped before she could hold it back.

Aimee shook it off. The best thing she could do for BethAnne was focus on finding the person responsible for her murder.

She had no intention of losing sight of the fact.

"Let's go out the front," she said.

Tanner nodded before retrieving a pair of running shoes. "I always keep a spare in my rucksack, in case my boots get trashed while I'm out on the land."

"That's a good idea," she said. "I thought you guys still rode horseback at Firebrand. For some reason, I thought BethAnne told me that. She talked about you all the time. You know that, right?" She was testing the waters to see if he'd figured her cousin out.

His face twisted in confusion. "No. I didn't. We used to get together more but haven't been as close in the past year."

"Really?"

"You sound surprised," he said. "Why is that?"

Should she tell him? This seemed like an opportune

time. Except that maybe this was one secret Aimee should hang onto.

"No reason," she said. "I know the two of you were close."

"Kind of," he said. "But not so much recently. Like I said, not in the past year or so. I was in a relationship that didn't end well, and I didn't want to spend a whole lot of time with people afterward."

"Oh, really?"

"What's that look about?" he asked, studying her again.

"No," she said, deciding it could wait. "It's all good. BethAnne just made it seem like the two of you spent a lot of time together."

"An occasional dinner out, sure," he confirmed. "But I wouldn't say we were best friends. Not like the two of you anyway."

BethAnne's assertions that she might start dating Tanner soon struck Aimee as odd, given this conversation. Wishful thinking on her cousin's part? Not that it mattered anymore.

"I can't imagine life without BethAnne," she admitted, redirecting her thoughts. "It's going to be so strange moving forward without her."

He reached out for her hand and then gave a gentle squeeze of reassurance. "I can't fathom how hard this must be for you. All I can say is that I'm here. You're not alone and you don't have to go through any of this on your own."

Why did those last words make her want to cry?

"I appreciate it," she said, taking a cool approach. Because falling apart wasn't an option, BethAnne needed Aimee to be strong, so she would be.

And, maybe, they would find some answers across the street.

7

Tanner held onto Aimee's hand as they crossed the street to Mrs. Weller's home. The lights were on even though it was still daylight outside. The blinds were cracked, allowing a peek of light.

Aimee rang the doorbell, which also had a camera on it. He wondered how those things worked. Could it record activity from across the street? Maybe they could ask about it. If there was a recording, life might become a lot easier.

The door opened a crack. "Aimee?"

"Yes, ma'am."

The door swung open wide. Mrs. Weller had to be nearing seventy years old. She was tall and sturdy. "Who is this handsome man you brought with you?"

Aimee's smile morphed. She seemed like she was struggling to hold back her emotions. "This is Tanner Firebrand, ma'am."

"BethAnne's Tanner?" Mrs. Weller asked with a wink and a twinkle in her eye. He wondered what that was about. Tanner made a mental note to ask what that meant later when he and Aimee were alone again. Mrs. Weller's enthusiasm at hearing his name caught him off guard.

"Yes," Aimee said with a small smile.

"Ma'am," Tanner said.

Mrs. Weller offered a smile before leaning into Aimee to whisper something he couldn't quite catch.

Aimee smiled in return and nodded. Her cheeks turned a few shades of red and she refused to look over at Tanner.

"Well, come on in," Mrs. Weller insisted, opening the door wide and breaking the moment of tension happening. "I've been wondering when BethAnne was coming home. Didn't realize she'd made the drive to Austin. Where is her car?"

"I'm afraid this isn't a social visit," Aimee started. She exhaled. He reached for her hand like he'd done several times before under similar circumstances, but she pulled hers away the second he made contact.

The rejection stung more than he cared to admit. In fact, he tried to convince himself it didn't matter one bit. His heart betrayed him with other ideas.

"Oh?" Mrs. Weller stood tall at what he guessed to be around five-feet-nine-inches. She would be considered sturdy by most standards. She had a head full of white hair that was piled on top of her head in a loose bun. Her eyebrows creased with concern as she stepped onto the porch and then closed the door behind her. "Is everything okay?"

"No, ma'am, it isn't," Aimee said, emotion causing her voice to crack. "I'm sorry, but I have to ask a few questions before I can tell you what's going on. Is that okay?"

"Yes, hon, go ahead," Mrs. Weller encouraged. "Ask whatever you need to. I don't mind one bit."

Aimee twisted her fingers together. "Have you seen anyone hanging around BethAnne's house lately?"

"Other than the usual?" the older woman asked.

"When you say usual...who do you mean?"

"Well, the doc stops by after work a few times a week but that's nothing new," Mrs. Weller said. Her gaze unfocused like she was looking deep inside herself for answers.

"Did he come by this week too?" Aimee asked. The use of calving rope didn't gel with the doctor being responsible, but it was curious that he stopped by several times a week after work. The doc was married, which meant he could be having an affair with BethAnne if they were seeing each other after hours and at her home.

"Like clockwork," Mrs. Weller informed. "I always left them alone to talk when he was over there."

"Why was that?" Aimee dug deeper.

"Oh, you know, they were discussing work stuff that didn't interest me," Mrs. Weller explained. She laughed. "I thought the two of them were having an affair for the longest time, but BethAnne swore they weren't."

"She never mentioned him to me or the fact that he stopped by so often," Aimee admitted.

"No?" Mrs. Weller said. "There might not have been much to tell. Routine work was how BethAnne put it when I cornered her on the topic. Of course, if they actually were having an affair, I doubt she'd tell me one way or the other. She would have enough sense to be embarrassed, considering his marital status."

"I know my cousin had her eye on someone," Aimee said, choosing her words carefully. Why was that? "It never occurred to me that she might be seeing her boss."

Mrs. Weller swiped at the air. "I wouldn't put a whole lot of credence to her and the doc sneaking around. He's fifteen years older than her. The two of them would make an odd pairing."

The pregnancy paper at her home made more sense if they were secretly working on fertility cases. There were too many missing puzzle pieces to make any real guesses at this point. It was like throwing a dart at the wall with a blindfold on. They had to start somewhere, though. An affair with her boss would give Dr. Carrol motive to keep her quiet if she threatened to tell his wife.

Wasn't that one of the biggest motives for murder? If someone else had figured out the affair, sewing BethAnne's mouth shut as a warning of what would happen to anyone else who threatened to talk would be effective.

It was possible Dr. Carrol was having an affair with someone else. BethAnne might have threatened to expose him. Or maybe there were under-the-table fertility cases? These made more sense than BethAnne having an affair with the older man to Tanner's thinking. Then again, maybe he didn't want to see his friend in that light.

Life had taught Tanner that anything was possible, and even the folks he believed he knew like the back of his hand could shock him with their actions. He'd learned not to make assumptions about anyone, even if he thought he knew them and especially if they were blood-related.

Speaking of which, he needed to check in on the situation at home. His mother had been cleared to move to Houston, where she had a better chance of receiving a fair trial. He needed to check in with the family to see if there was anything he should be doing. He'd given his brother Rowan a hard time for abandoning the family during a crisis, and Tanner might be around, but he'd mentally checked out recently, which brought on another wave of guilt that he wasn't doing his part.

"Does the camera at the front door record across the street?" Tanner asked.

"It's a fake," Mrs. Weller admitted. "But don't tell anyone."

"What about other cars or trucks parked in front of BethAnne's house?" Aimee continued as he tuned back into the conversation.

"Now that you mention it, there was a car parked outside her house a couple of nights ago," Mrs. Weller said after a thoughtful pause. "It was dark, so I couldn't tell you what color, but it was one of those…how do you call it?" She shot a helpless look toward Tanner and then Aimee. And then it must've dawned on her. "Muscle cars."

"A hotrod?" Aimee asked.

"That's right," the older woman said with a self-satisfied smile. "It had to have been navy blue or black, something dark like that."

"Doesn't ring any bells for me," Aimee said before turning to him. "What about you?"

"No," he admitted. But at least this gave them a direction even if it wasn't much to go on. The doctor and an affair—with someone, and it didn't have to be BethAnne—resonated.

Was it too obvious? Or was the easy answer the right one?

∾

"What happened to BethAnne?" Mrs. Weller asked, point blank. She put a balled fist on her hip. "I'm a big girl. I can take it."

"The sheriff isn't releasing a whole lot of details—"

Mrs. Weller's hand came up to cover her heart as she gasped. "Is she...?"

Aimee nodded as one of those rogue tears escaped, falling down her cheek.

"Oh, hon. I'm so sorry." Mrs. Weller pulled Aimee into a hug. "I had no idea anything like this was possible in our little town, despite all the recent gossip about a crime wave hitting Lone Star Pass. We've all been locking our doors, including BethAnne. I fussed at her the other week for leaving her keys in her car like we all used to do."

Aimee gently untangled herself from the well-meaning neighbor. "It's certainly a shock to lose her, especially in this way."

"Your cousin was a dear," Mrs. Weller said as big teardrops fell, staining her frock. "She was one of the kindest people I've ever met."

"She was," Aimee said, still getting used to referring to BethAnne in the past tense. Would she ever truly adjust to not having her best friend around?

"I'll keep my eye on the place to see if the sonofabitch returns," Mrs. Weller promised.

Aimee needed to warn her about the sheriff. "The sheriff might come by and ask a few questions. He doesn't want us interfering with his investigation, which we understand. But—"

"She's your family." Mrs. Weller huffed as she crossed her arms over her chest. "The sheriff has no right to tell you not to try to find out what happened."

"He doesn't quite see it that way," Aimee pointed out.

"You came over to borrow milk," she said, throwing her hands up in the air. "How silly of me to keep you standing here talking on the porch. Hold on and I'll go get some. Stay right here." With a wink, Mrs. Weller disappeared into the house.

Aimee reached for Tanner's hand but he folded his arms over his chest, keeping it out of reach. He shot her a look. It took her a second to realize what was going on. Right. She'd rejected his hand in front of Mrs. Weller. "I'm sorry for—"

The door opening cut her off.

Mrs. Weller held out a jar filled with milk. "Here you go. Don't worry about paying it back. I'll head over when I need something."

Aimee took the offering. "Thank you, ma'am."

"Go on now," the older woman said with a sniffle. She managed a genuine smile. "Get out of here before the sheriff comes."

Aimee nodded.

"Wish we could have met under different circumstances," Tanner said, extending a hand.

Mrs. Weller shook his hand. "BethAnne always spoke so highly of you. It's nice to finally meet. I think we both agree about the nature of the circumstances. I'm sorry the two of you never..." She caught herself as Aimee shot a warning look. "Well, let's just say that I feel like I already know you, and if you ever need anything I hope you'll consider me like family. Don't be a stranger."

"Same to you," Tanner said with the kind of charm Aimee was certain brought out a smile with everyone he met. "And I certainly will keep in touch."

Aimee turned first and almost ran smack into the middle of his chest. He was unreadable now. A wall had come up between them. Tanner Firebrand didn't take rejection well. To be fair, did anyone?

"At least we have a car now," she said when they crossed the street and headed toward his truck.

He opened the door for her and then held out a hand so she could climb in.

"I can put the milk away if you give me the key," he said to her.

"The fact we're leaving probably blows our cover," she replied. "That whole charade must have been so Mrs. Weller could honestly say we stopped by for milk. That way, she wouldn't be lying if he asked about us."

"I wouldn't want to be on her bad side," Tanner said. "She's cunning."

"Does she have one, though?"

"Probably not," he said before closing the door and then rounding the front of the vehicle. He claimed the driver's seat and then started the engine. "What was Mrs. Weller talking about? Did BethAnne tell her that we were a couple?"

Aimee didn't like the idea of giving away her cousin's secret because there was no point now. Then again, what was the point of keeping it secret? The cat was almost out of the bag. When Tanner had time to process the information, he would come up with the answer on his own. She might as well spill the beans. "BethAnne was in love with you, Tanner. You didn't know that?"

"What? No? There's no w—" His mouth opened and then clamped shut again. The puzzle pieces were coming together in his mind.

"That's right. She was head over heels for you and swore everyone to secrecy who knew," she said. "I'm pretty sure she was planning your wedding."

"What does that do to the theory she might have been having an affair with her boss?" he asked. Of all the questions he could have asked, this one surprised her. But then, he probably needed a minute to digest the information.

Clearly, he'd been caught off guard. And it must feel odd to be the last one to find out someone was in love with him.

"I mean, I don't think it's out of the question she would have an affair with her boss," she pointed out. "I'd like to think it's unlikely. I'd like to think she wouldn't do that to another woman. She certainly didn't mention anything about it to me, not that she would if it was happening. She would have enough sense to be embarrassed."

He sat there, chewing on the information.

"Plus, it wasn't like the two of you were dating," she continued when he didn't speak up. "So, it wouldn't be any sort of betrayal in that sense."

"An affair with a married man doesn't sit right with me," he said. "But then, a positive pregnancy test belonging to her doesn't feel right either."

"You heard what Mrs. Weller said. Apparently, the doctor came over several times a week after work."

"I wonder what he told his wife," Tanner said. "There had to be a reason for his actions, even if it was a lie."

Aimee exhaled. "Maybe we'll get answers at the office." Now that the cat was out of the bag about BethAnne's feelings for Tanner, she wondered how that would change things.

8

Tanner white-knuckled the steering wheel. He, of all people, should know folks kept secrets. So, maybe it shouldn't surprise him that his friend might have had a secret life that included having an affair with a married man or the fact that she'd been in love with him. Both shocked the hell out of him because he thought he knew her. "I hate secrets."

"I'm sorry that I didn't tell you about BethAnne before," Aimee said. "It didn't feel like my secret to tell. Plus, she's gone now, and I guess I didn't think it mattered much. I'm also sorry that you had to find out through Mrs. Weller."

"She didn't mean anything by it," he pointed out. The older woman was the type to look out for those around her. She was a good person.

"She wasn't exactly subtle."

"That she wasn't," he agreed. Normally, he would have a good laugh about something like this, but nothing was very funny after seeing what had happened to BethAnne. "I thought the two of us were good friends. That's all. I never had any interest in anything else, and I was honest about it.

In fact, we both talked about it and agreed we would always be better off as friends, so I guess I'm a little deer-in-headlights about it all."

"She thought you'd come around eventually and realize the two of you were meant to be together," Aimee said. "The way she talked about how the two of you keep in touch and check in on each other made it seem possible, but I'd only ever heard one side of the story."

"There was never anything more than friendship on my side," he repeated, just to be clear. He never would have kissed Aimee if he'd had feelings for her cousin. That would have been all kinds of wrong in his book. "I don't know where she got the idea that we could be anything more."

"You're honest to a fault," Aimee said. "After spending time with you, it's easy to see you would never lead someone on."

"No, I wouldn't." As much as he appreciated the vote of confidence and the compliment, rejection didn't sit well with him. "There's no reason to lead anyone on. I don't need a cheerleading camp, and I prefer to be around folks who are honest with me."

His pulse was rising, so he needed to calm down.

"The heart wants what it wants, Tanner."

"Is that an excuse to lie to someone you're supposed to be friends with? Because no relationship, friend or otherwise, can survive on a foundation of dishonesty."

"I agree," Aimee said. "You and BethAnne had a lot of history and I don't think she wanted to lose the friendship."

"So she would rather sit back and pine for someone, talk about the person with just about everyone else, than come to me and ask? I could have set her straight if she was confused," he stated.

"And then what?"

"What do you mean?" he asked.

"If she came to you and said she was madly in love with you, are you telling me that you would still be able to look at her and see friendship?"

Tanner had to think about that one for a minute. "No. I guess not. I'd like to think that I could, but it would linger once it was out of the bag."

"That's why she wasn't ready to say anything yet. She was scared to lose the friendship, the history. She tried to manage her feelings by dating other people when someone interesting came along, but no one measured up to you," Aimee explained.

"We would have eventually worked it out," he said. "The friendship side."

"Not without it getting messy first."

Well, he really couldn't argue there.

"She said you'd recently been in a relationship and—"

"Why is it you seem to know so much about me and I have almost nothing on you from BethAnne?" he asked.

"It's not like you're all we ever talked about," she said a little defensively.

"I wasn't implying that."

"BethAnne brought you up from time to time," she continued. "I encouraged her to tell you how she felt, by the way. I thought you deserved to know and I didn't like her pining over someone who wasn't into her."

"But she didn't listen," he stated the obvious.

"No, she didn't," Aimee said. "But I think we both know how stubborn BethAnne could be when she wants to. And she always made it seem like the door was cracked when it came to the two of you."

"Stubborn as a mule, she was," he said on a laugh. It caught him off guard that he would find anything funny given the circumstance, but humor was a good way to ease some of the tension they both were feeling.

Aimee laughed too, and his damn fool heart squeezed.

"Folks are complicated," he finally said. He'd had no idea that BethAnne had been in love with him. Shouldn't there have been clues? How hard could it be to figure out?

"*Life* is complicated," she added.

With a mother in prison for attempted murder, he knew a thing or two about life going off the rails. As far as his friendship with BethAnne, he wished she'd been able to talk to him about what was going on. What kind of relationship did they have if they couldn't be honest with each other?

Not a minute later, he turned into the parking lot of Dr. Carrol's practice. He'd picked BethAnne up here a handful of times so the place was familiar.

"She loved her job," Aimee said, breaking into his thoughts.

"And she was good at it too," he pointed out. Those were facts.

He parked in a spot near the back of the small lot. The one-story, red brick building housed a bustling practice. There were at least fifteen vehicles parked in the lot. The front door opened and a pregnant woman walked out. She got into her vehicle and pulled out of the lot and was replaced almost immediately by another car.

"We should probably discuss what we want to ask once we get inside and who we want to talk to," Tanner said.

"No offense, but I think I should take the lead with Dr. Carrol."

"Why is that?" he asked.

"Because you're big and strong, and he might feel intimidated by you," she pointed out. He'd take it as a compliment.

"He might feel less threatened if the questions come from a woman."

"Okay," he agreed. Although Aimee was formidable. "It also might make more sense coming from a relative."

"True enough." She unbuckled her seatbelt but didn't make a move to get out. "One of her work friends is named Missy. I think we should definitely talk to her to get a sense of what she knows, if anything."

"I've heard of Missy," he said. "There was something about the woman that BethAnne didn't trust."

"Really?" Aimee sounded surprised.

"I'm pretty sure she was talking about Missy when she said she couldn't tell her anything beyond the surface," he informed.

"Strange, because I could have sworn BethAnne said the opposite."

"Guess we'll find out in a minute," he said. "The sheriff might have already been here."

She shook her head. "I'm certain he is working the evidence and still dealing with my aunt and uncle."

"Okay, then. Let's poke around and see what comes out." The thought occurred to him that asking questions could be dangerous. Someone had used BethAnne to make a threat. Would the person come after him? Aimee?

They were about to find out.

~

TANNER CAME AROUND and opened the door for Aimee before offering a hand. She took the offering and he immediately withdrew his hand from hers. The message was clear. He was being polite. Otherwise, he wasn't interested in physical contact.

As they walked toward the double glass doors, she held back the urge to reach for him. Instead, she thought about what questions she might ask Dr. Carrol when they came face-to-face. Would a doctor have access to a calving rope?

A cowboy or rancher made more sense. Then again, Tanner had said that kind of rope would be readily available in these parts. The doctor, if he was responsible for BethAnne's murder, would most likely be able to get his hands on some without much effort. Heck, half the pickups in the parking lot most likely had rope in the bed of their truck. How difficult would it be to snag some?

What question should she start with? The obvious one she wanted to ask wasn't an option. Walking straight into his office and asking if he killed BethAnne would most likely get them thrown out on their backsides.

Having Tanner with her looked like she was bringing muscle.

Aimee had only waved at the doctor from across the parking lot when she'd picked up her cousin. She'd been inside the building before but stayed up in the reception area. It's the reason she knew Missy. They'd talked while Aimee waited for BethAnne to get off work a handful of times over the years.

Of course, this would all be a lot easier if Aimee had come back to Lone Star Pass more often. Austin had live music and a hopping single vibe with all the young college students. It was half the reason BethAnne wanted to come to Aimee rather than the other way around.

And BethAnne might have been wanting to take a breather from being around the man she loved who wasn't into her...Tanner.

At least Tanner was good through and through. Aimee couldn't vouch for the doctor. Would she know if the man was evil by looking straight into his eyes? Could she handle being in the same room with her cousin's killer without losing it and going off on the man?

What about the car Mrs. Weller had seen? Aimee had scanned the parking lot for signs of it. Came up empty.

As Tanner opened the door, Aimee's cell buzzed. She reached into her purse and checked the screen. She tilted it so Tanner could see for himself before motioning to stay outside to take the call.

"Yes, Sheriff," she said after answering. She turned her back to the glass door and held her breath.

"Your aunt and uncle are here in my office," he began.

"Sheriff, you didn't call me to tell me that," she said.

"No, I didn't." He was stalling and she didn't like it one bit. "I thought you might like to be here with them when I deliver the news."

"What news?"

"I think you should come into the office," he hedged.

"There's no time for that, Sheriff. I'd rather know what's going on right now if that's okay with you."

"It's about the victim," he continued after a pause. "BethAnne Dyer was approximately eight weeks pregnant at the time of her death."

Aimee's knees almost buckled. Her cousin hadn't said a word to her about her pregnancy. Hell, Aimee hadn't even known BethAnne was dating anyone. Of course, accidents happened all the time. Condoms broke. Although rarely. More likely they came off in the heat of the moment, than actually broke.

"Are you aware of anyone Ms. Dyer was dating or having a romantic relationship with?" he asked.

"We've already covered that ground," she admitted. "If I knew, I would have told you already." The man her cousin was deeply in love with happened to be standing next to Aimee, so she really was confused.

What other secrets did BethAnne have? An affair with a married man? He might kill her to stop her from telling his wife about the two of them. Then, there was the baby to consider. Get rid of BethAnne and it stands to reason the baby goes with her. The urge to cry was replaced with the urge to scream.

"I apologize for you having to find out this way," the sheriff said, his voice filled with compassion.

"Thank you."

"Also, my office is looking deeper into phone records," he confirmed.

Tanner's name would come up. Was that at least part of the reason the sheriff wanted them to come into his office? So he could casually, or not so casually, question Tanner?

"Thank you for the information," she said. "Tanner and I will stop by your office in an hour or so. I'd like to visit with my aunt and uncle while they're still there."

"I believe they'd like that," the sheriff said. "Are you and Tanner still together?"

She wasn't sure she liked the question. "Yes, sir."

"And he'll be coming with you to my office?" he continued.

"Yes, sir."

"Good," he said. "It'll save me the trouble of bringing him in."

Aimee felt the blood rush from her face. "I'll be sure to let him know."

She ended the call and then filled Tanner in on the details. All the color drained from his face at the pregnancy news. He muttered a string of curses aimed at no one in particular. She could relate because those same words came to mind when she thought about the circumstances of her cousin's murder.

"It's not surprising my name would come up in the investigation," Tanner finally said when he found his voice again. "Think about it. BethAnne and I spoke from time to time. She texted me. Although, I have to admit that I'm bad about returning those. I usually pick up the phone to make a call. If someone texts, I'm liable to call them back rather than respond."

"Not to mention, anyone close to her knew that she had feelings for you," Aimee pointed out. "Now that I think about it, I'd be surprised if he didn't call you in for questioning. Although you were there on the scene trying to help find her just as much as I was."

"From what I've read and heard, murderers often show up in search parties," he said on a frustrated exhale. "Apparently, it's part of the thrill of getting away with the crime."

"It's disgusting, is what it is."

"Agreed," he said before clenching his back teeth. His jaw muscle ticked. "Let's go talk to a real suspect." Tanner nodded toward the doctor's office.

Aimee inhaled a deep breath and squared her shoulders. Maybe they could get answers inside.

9

Tanner opened the door to Dr. Carrol's lobby area. Side-by-side, blue chairs lined the walls. The white tile flooring gave a hospital-like effect. Light beige walls completed the look. Art in the form of pregnant women cradling bumps and mothers holding babies in abstract paintings hung on the walls. An enclosed reception desk sat directly opposite the door. There was a bar-height counter with an opened appointment book on the visitor's side of the partition. Next to the book was a cup full of pens. A glass partition went counter to ceiling height. Behind it, there was a lady working the phone and a couple of nurses shuffling around with files in their hands.

Missy worked in billing. She was the one who checked patients out. That much Tanner remembered from his conversations with BethAnne. He was interested in her career, but office gossip went in one ear and out the other. She wasn't the kind of person who sat around and bad-mouthed folks, so much as providing updates on how everyone around her was doing along with what they were up to.

BethAnne was a talker, so it surprised him even more that she had secrets—especially a secret pregnancy. She didn't tell him that her boss was stopping by after work so often. And what about the muscle car? She didn't generally get involved with someone who took risks, like someone who drove a fast car might. She didn't hang with the Red Bull-drinking crowd. Then, there was the pregnancy that she'd been hiding for weeks.

He reached for Aimee's arm as they walked up to the counter. Another familiar face sat on the other side of the glass on a call. Carly glanced up and immediately put the call on hold. She opened the partition.

"BethAnne didn't show up for work, and she didn't call," Carly said. "Is everything okay? It's not like her to miss work like this."

This line of questioning meant the sheriff hadn't stopped by or sent a deputy yet. That was probably a good thing for them. He gently squeezed Aimee's arm. She responded with an almost imperceptible nod.

Aimee cleared her throat, clearly stalling for time. "It's good to see you, Carly."

"Yeah, you too."

"My cousin is going to be out for a while," Aimee explained.

"Why is that? Is everything okay?" Carly asked. Small-town folks were notorious for getting into each other's business. Mostly, the intrusions into each other's personal business was well-intentioned. Folks in Lone Star Pass would bring over soup if someone was under the weather. Or make it a point to check on someone who was going through a rough patch.

Of course, there was another side to the coin. Folks could be too nosy, as far as he was concerned, and give into gossip behind someone's back. His side of the family had been victim of small-minded judgment. That was the part he didn't like so much. It didn't seem like news about BethAnne was out yet. The sheriff would appreciate it since he wanted to keep things quiet for the time being.

"Yes," Aimee reassured. "BethAnne will be fine. It's the reason I came to town. I'm here to make sure she has everything she needs and is well taken care of."

"A lot has been going around lately," Carly said as she reached under the counter and then pulled out a mask. She held it up. "Working in a medical environment, you'd think I'd be better about wearing one of these."

Aimee smiled. For winging it, she was doing a decent job. "Do you mind if we come around and pick up a few things from BethAnne's desk at the nurse's station?"

"It's probably okay," Carly said. She shot a look that said the two of them should probably be wearing masks, after she returned hers to the spot underneath the counter where she must have it on a hook.

Missy walked into view to grab a chart and call a patient back to get insurance information. She glanced at the window and her eyes widened. Tanner got that reaction from folks from time to time being a Firebrand, but he would never get used to it. Still, this time felt different.

The minute her gaze shifted to Aimee, Missy set the file down and made a beeline for the door. She came into the lobby where half a dozen patients waited, and walked straight to them.

"BethAnne isn't answering any of my calls or responding to my texts," Missy said as she gave Aimee a quick hug. She turned toward Tanner next. "I'm Missy, by the way."

"Tanner Firebrand," he said before offering a handshake.

"I know who you are," Missy said. He recognized the tone. Judgement. It was a shame he couldn't escape his family's reputation but not altogether unexpected. "BethAnne mentioned you a few times. Plus, I've seen you in the parking lot a couple of times."

Maybe he'd been the one to snap to judgment. "I remember seeing you before. Sorry we didn't get a chance to meet."

"No problem," Missy said. "BethAnne talked about you so much I feel like I already know you." Her gaze shifted to Aimee. "Speaking of your cousin, where is she?"

Tanner noticed a difference in Carly's response to them being there. Missy didn't look him in the eye despite being somewhat familiar with him. A few red flags went up with her initial reaction to seeing them. She'd come across as scared. Or maybe it was just that she was a little too surprised they were there. Or that it was them. Was she expecting someone else to show?

The sheriff, maybe?

"My cousin isn't herself right now," Aimee explained with a frown. "She's down sick." Her voice raised when she lied and she shifted her weight from her left to right foot, but he didn't think Missy caught on.

In fact, she checked behind her like she didn't want someone to see her speaking to them at all. Another red flag.

Carly realized she'd left someone on hold all this time. With a start, she picked up the receiver and apologized.

At this point, he wished they could spend five minutes alone with Missy. He had a feeling they could get information out of her. What did she know?

Aimee leaned an elbow on the counter, forcing a smile to act casual. She was probably failing but the saying *fake it 'til you make it* came to mind. Her heart thundered in her chest. She'd never been a good liar, but too much was on the line to go back now. She wanted to keep her lies as close to the truth as possible in order to sell them. Guilt slapped her, but she reminded herself of the stakes. A killer was on the loose. Someone who could, in theory, kill again. Someone who had, most definitely, killed her cousin. She needed to think of a reason to access her cousin's workspace and fast. "I was hoping to go through BethAnne's desk while I'm here."

Missy's eyebrow shot up.

"She left a couple of her favorite things," Aimee clarified. "There's a travel mug she's obsessed with and—"

Panic set in and her mind went blank.

"There's a tea that she orders off the internet," Tanner interjected. "She keeps a supply here at work."

Thank the stars for his quick thinking because Missy smiled and nodded. "It's that one special tea she literally throws herself in front of the cabinet when I try to sneak it, isn't it?"

"Yeah, that one," Tanner confirmed with a smile. Missy practically melted under his gaze. Granted, the man was charming. He was gorgeous too. More importantly, he was intelligent. He could hold his own in any conversation, which meant more than a pretty face. Don't get her wrong, she had nothing against good looks, and his were especially easy on the eyes. But his intelligence made him the real deal. And his quick thinking just saved the day. "BethAnne usually keeps it stocked at home, but she's been slipping lately."

"It's probably from all the stress she's been under," Missy confided. "Come with me."

In the next couple of seconds, they were being led back to the patient rooms and nurses' station.

"The place isn't the same without BethAnne," Missy continued as she walked them to the back.

"She talks about you all the time too," Tanner added. "How's your mother, by the way?"

"Oh, you know, she's getting older," Missy said, lowering her voice. Tanner was putting her at ease. But then, he had a way about him that caused those around him to relax. All he had to do was smile to get the opposite sex's attention.

Aimee had no right to be jealous but it was easy to see why BethAnne had fallen for the man. One of his best qualities was that he didn't seem aware of how easily women fell at his feet.

"Right here is BethAnne's spot," Missy said, pointing to a cabinet. "I have the key right here." She searched a pocket and then another before locating a small ring with a couple of keys on it. "Here we go." She unlocked the cabinet and then took a step back. "Take whatever you want."

"Thank you," Aimee said before grabbing a box of the special chocolate peppermint tea her cousin loved. She took the travel mug next. There was a pink lipstick smudge on the rim. Aimee had to take in a breath to stop the flood of tears threatening. Too much emotion would invite questions Aimee couldn't answer without giving up the rouse. She cleared her throat. "This will make her happy."

"I can walk you out to the parking lot," Missy said. She seemed a little too eager to get them out of the building. It might also mean she wanted to tell Aimee something—something important?

"Is the doctor in?" Tanner asked.

Missy's face turned sheet-white. What was that about?

"I think he took off a minute ago," Missy lied as she

leaned against the nurses' station. The move blocked a door that Aimee was certain led into the doctor's office. Why? "No one is supposed to be back here, so we better head back to the front before I get in trouble." She shot a half-felt smile. "Can't afford to lose my job."

If the doctor was nowhere around, who would chew her out? Plus, there were too many patients in the waiting room for Aimee to buy the line about the doctor leaving. Since Missy looked like she'd jump out of her skin if someone said *boo,* Aimee decided not to push the nervous nurse.

"Lead the way," Aimee said to her. Tanner reached for her hand, linked their fingers, and squeezed.

No, they didn't come all this way to be walked out the front door. Aimee needed to think of an excuse to stay back here.

"Mind if I used the ladies' room before we get back on the road?" Aimee asked Missy, hoping her restroom excuse would buy them some time. She had a feeling the doctor would show up if they stuck around long enough. Missy was trying to rush them out for a reason. If the doctor wasn't in the building, there was no way the nurse would get into trouble. She was lying or hiding something.

"Um, sure," Missy said, stopping mid-hallway. She pointed to a door to her left. "It's right there."

"Thank you," Aimee said. "My bladder is about to burst after drinking a venti iced coffee on the way over."

"I know the feeling, girl," Missy said. Her voice might be casual but the muscles in her face were pulled taut with tension.

Aimee headed into the bathroom. How long could she stall? Hide inside? Hopefully, long enough to give Tanner time to dig around with Missy. It was time for him to pull out that Firebrand charm. She'd known a few of his relatives, but she couldn't say who was a brother or who was a cousin. The family had eighteen between the two sides, all men according to BethAnne. Of course, her cousin had believed Tanner was the special one out of the bunch. Aimee didn't need to meet the others to know just how special he was.

The low hum of voices outside the door said he was at least trying to work some magic. It was frustrating to be this close to the doctor and yet feel so far away from any real answers.

She checked her phone and then flushed the toilet. Fake washing her hands came next before she couldn't think of a reason to stay in the bathroom any longer. Listening at the door, she strained to hear what Missy was saying to Tanner.

Words were too hard to make out, but Missy's voice had raised a couple of octaves like a woman's does when she's flirting with someone. Again, Aimee had no designs on Tanner so none of this should bother her as much as it did. He was a grown man capable of deciding who he wanted to date and who he didn't. The fact she'd kissed him—and he'd thoroughly kissed her back—shouldn't weigh in one way or the other. She'd been stressed beyond belief after what happened to BethAnne. In some ways, Aimee was relieved to be on the scene to get answers about what happened to her cousin.

But actually seeing what had happened was also the reason Aimee was sick to her stomach.

She opened the door to Missy cozied up to Tanner. He didn't seem fazed one bit by the closeness, even when Missy just flipped her hair back and batted her eyelashes. Definite flirting moves if Aimee had ever seen them.

"I can't imagine why BethAnne would go hiking of all things," Missy said. "And to have to call out a search party because she got lost." She paused. "Well, that part actually does sound like BethAnne. It would be just like her to lose her way in the woods because she was most definitely not an outdoorsy girl."

"She should have called me," Tanner said, looking up and straight while Missy stared up at his eyes with a look of appreciation. "I've been on just about every trail in Texas at one time or another. Spent a good portion of my youth out camping in various places."

"Oh, that must have been cool," Missy said. She was so wrapped up in Tanner, that she seemed to forget all about Aimee in the bathroom. She stood in the doorway across the hall, not ten feet from where Missy stood talking to Tanner.

"I came home with my fair share of poison ivy," he admitted with a laugh. Aimee could tell he was forcing conversation and charm, but Missy was too caught in his spell to notice or care.

Aimee didn't dare interfere with the conversation. This might be small talk but Missy could slip up. Aimee had a feeling Tanner was biding his time, waiting for the right moment to ask the right question.

"The last time I asked for a file, you brought it two hours later," a familiar male voice barked at a nurse who walked beside him. "I needed it right then, not hours after the fact."

"Looks like Dr. Carrol came back," Aimee said to Missy.

The billing clerk's face turned red. "I didn't realize the doctor was still here."

He made a beeline for his office with the aid practically jogging to keep up with him. The man walked with purpose, she'd give him that.

And he was about to explain why he made so many after-work trips to her cousin's house if Aimee had anything to say about it.

10

Tanner made a beeline for the doctor, whose back was turned. "Dr. Carrol, my friend and I would like to have a word with you in private."

The doctor turned around, and for a split second his eyes widened when he saw Aimee. He brought his hand up to smooth down a perfect tie. A nervous tick? "I have cases stacked up today. I'm afraid I—"

Tanner hooked his arm in the doctor's and walked toward the door with a gold plaque that had the good doctor's name engraved in it. "It wasn't a request." He could hear the almost growl-like quality in his tone. The doctor reacted by his body tensing.

"Am I allowed to know what this is about?" he managed to ask after a few steps forward. He seemed to know better than to argue at this point.

"You'll find out once we go inside, unless you want the entire office to hear your personal business." Tanner lowered his voice. "And everyone to hear the real reason you stopped by BethAnne's several times a week after office hours."

The doctor shook his head and complied. He had to be roughly six feet tall, so significantly shorter than Tanner, with a runner's build. He had sandy-blond hair that had a Kennedy look to it. In fact, this guy looked like he would fit right into the famous political family. He had the perfectly straight white teeth and tanned skin they all seemed to have. And the effortless look and charisma of a Kennedy male that was famous for seducing women from all walks of life.

Tanner figured most women would see the doctor as good-looking. He had an air of authority, of being better than everyone else, that attracted some. Arrogant was the term that came to mind. Nose in the air. The man had money considering his thriving practice.

The minute the trio stepped inside the office, Tanner closed the door. He'd planned on letting Aimee take the lead on this part, but staring in the face of the man who might be responsible for a heinous act of murder sent white-hot anger racing through Tanner.

He jerked Dr. Carrol's arm around, slamming his back into the closed door with a loud thump.

"How long was the affair going on, Robert?" he demanded, picking up Dr. Carrol's first name from the gold plaque. It was fitting with the Kennedy comparison.

Robert shook his head. His face twisted in agony. "I'm a bad husband. My wife didn't deserve what I did to her."

Interesting that he had no plans to deny the affair. Would he be so honest if he knew BethAnne had been murdered? It didn't stand to reason he would, considering he had to know this admission would put him squarely in the position of prime suspect. Sewing BethAnne's mouth shut was a warning for someone else not to speak up.

Robert's actions seemed extreme under the circumstances but he had a lot to lose if he got divorced.

"If word got out you were having an affair with one of your nurses, your business would be ruined," Tanner surmised. "There's no husband in the county who would allow a good-looking doctor like you to have unfettered access to his wife, is there?"

The more he thought about it, the more it made sense.

Robert's face twisted in confusion. "Is that what you think I care about? I'd have nothing if not for my wife. The only person I care about protecting is her." Desperation reeked. "How much is it going to take?"

"To what?" Tanner asked. From the corner of his eye, he saw Aimee circling around behind Robert's desk.

"To keep this little secret between the three of us?" Robert asked like it was a serious consideration on Tanner's part. Was this man out of his mind or that bold? Did he think he could throw money at the two of them to make all this go away?

"Do you know who I am?" Tanner asked, disgusted. He didn't normally throw around his family name, but money wasn't exactly a problem for him.

"Yes," Robert confirmed. "Which is exactly the reason I believed you would understand how important a person's reputation was in this town. Once lost, it could never be recovered."

"I thought you were worried about your wife finding out about your office affair," Tanner said.

Robert hunkered down as a look of panic crossed his features.

"What? Am I being too loud?" Tanner asked in dramatic fashion. This bastard cheated on his wife at the very least. He had an affair with one of his employees. Did he know about the pregnancy? Tanner bit back a curse. An inconvenient pregnancy would destroy this doctor's reputation. The affair would be bad enough. Robert was right about that. But an illegitimate child? That would bring even more shame down on his family and his medical practice. Considering the nature of his practice, trust was paramount.

"Tell BethAnne no one knows," Robert whispered like that would make Tanner lower his voice too. "She can come back to work. I'll give her a raise."

"Why would she want to look at your face ever again?" Tanner bit out.

"Even better," Robert said. "I'll give her a recommendation to work with a colleague in Austin. That way she'll be closer to her cousin. Everyone wins. Don't you see? This works for everyone." The desperation in Robert's voice had Tanner almost convinced the man had no idea BethAnne was dead. Or he might just be that slick.

Robert knew too much about BethAnne for her to have believed they were having a casual fling. She wasn't the kind to go around sleeping with married men. Not if she knew they were married. Pieces to this puzzle were still missing.

"Not a chance," Tanner said. "Everything will be out in the open soon enough and then what will happen to your practice?"

"I'd lose everything," Robert said. "Please. There has to be something you want to keep this a secret."

"All I want is the truth about what happened between you and BethAnne," Tanner insisted.

"I've told you al—"

"How did you convince her to sleep with you?" Tanner persisted.

"What makes you think—"

Tanner shot Robert a warning look that could freeze

hell. "Don't play with me, Robert. You won't win. This is the time to come clean about what you did to BethAnne." Tanner pressed the outside of his forearm against Robert's chest, pinning him to the door.

Robert's face twisted. Several emotions passed behind his eyes like a procession. Frustration. Fear. Anger. Resolve? "Yes, I talked her into having the affair. Is that what you want to hear?"

"If it's the truth," Tanner said, wondering how quickly this guy would crumble under the scrutiny of the sheriff's questions.

"She asked about my wife, but I said we were getting a divorce," Robert confessed. "BethAnne said she didn't want to be a rebound from my marriage but I told her that I'd been in love with her for years."

It took all Tanner's self-control not to deck this bastard.

"The truth is that I knew she was lonely and pining for a guy who wasn't available, so I told her what she wanted to hear," Robert admitted. "Does that make me a jerk? Yes. I can admit it. My wife and I were going through a rough patch and I needed comfort and companionship."

"Are you trying to say BethAnne was an easy mark?" Tanner asked through clenched teeth.

A hand slamming against the desk caused Robert to tense up again. He turned his head to the side as though it would be impossible to punch him and damage his face.

"No," he retracted. "All I'm saying is that most of the nurses have flirted with me but not her. She was a challenge."

Patience be damned, Tanner balled his right hand into a fist and decked the bastard. His head smacked the solid wooden door behind him and blood squirted from his nose. Tanner felt no sympathy for the guy.

Did that make him a jerk? Maybe. But BethAnne deserved so much more than a man intent on using her as some kind of challenge, getting her pregnant, and then throwing her away along with a warning to anyone else who knew about the affair not to speak up.

∼

AIMEE HAD HEARD MORE than she could stand. She came flying around the desk as Tanner's fist connected with the man's face. "You sonofabitch."

"You broke my nose," Robert accused Tanner, his once arrogant voice turned whiney now. Was this man capable of killing BethAnne, dragging her body, and sewing her mouth shut? He most definitely had a God complex; Aimee had heard that could come with the territory with doctors. Was he a killer?

"How does it feel to take advantage of someone who cared about you?" Aimee accused. "And then you think... what? That you can throw money at us to make the problem go away or beg us not to tell your wife or office about the affair. What a waste of a human being you turned out to be."

Did he know about the pregnancy? Was it the reason her cousin was strangled and thrown into a shallow grave?

"Where were you two days ago?" Aimee asked, figuring they might not have to drop the pregnancy or death bomb on him if he had an iron-clad alibi.

"Fishing," he supplied.

"Who'd you go with?" she pushed.

"No one," he said. "Fishing clears my mind and I've been under stress lately ever since..."

He stopped short of finishing the sentence.

"What?" Aimee asked. "My cousin threatened to tell

your wife?" Or did he mean the pregnancy? Aimee suppressed a gasp. What if BethAnne had told him about the pregnancy and he flipped out? It might explain the sudden hiking trip. He might have lured BethAnne out hiking so they could discuss how to handle the pregnancy. And then he—a familiar person—came up from behind. BethAnne might even think he was being sweet, coming up from behind to wrap his arms around her. But then he surprised her with a rope around her neck. He looked strong enough to pull it off. BethAnne wasn't more than five-feet-four-inches. The gym was to be avoided at all costs. Working out wasn't high on BethAnne's list. When Aimee had asked her cousin to go for a run, she'd asked if the police would be chasing them because that was the only reason a person should run in her book.

"We talked about keeping what we had between us a secret," Robert admitted. "I urged her not to go public with the affair."

"Is that when she figured out you'd been lying to her the whole time?" Aimee demanded to know. "Using her?"

"I wasn't," he tried to deny. "I was lonely. She was lonely. We had a good time together." He flinched when Tanner drew back his fist for the second time. "Don't hit me again. Please." Blood dripped from the doctor's nose onto his white lab coat. He wore gray slacks, a steel-gray shirt, and a silk tie.

Robert Carrol would be considered hot by most women's standards. He was a little too Kennedy-like in her book, a little too bronzed, too perfect. But then, Tanner Firebrand was more to her taste, and he was off limits despite sharing the sexiest kiss she'd ever experienced. She'd had a crush on him way back when, but he never looked twice at her. Until recently.

"I'm not going to strike you again," Tanner finally conceded. "Not unless you give me a good reason to."

Robert shook his head vigorously. How tough was he now when he was begging Tanner not to punch him? Was this man capable of murder?

"I won't," Robert promised. "Can we take a seat and discuss this like adults?" If BethAnne could see the man now, would she still be so enamored with him? The fact she hadn't so much as mentioned him to Aimee meant BethAnne was embarrassed. Despite his claims that his marriage was over, BethAnne had to realize on some level the man was lying to her. Right? BethAnne was sharp. But she was also vulnerable. It was one of her better qualities, actually. She wasn't hardened by the world.

A lightning bolt of anger shot through Aimee at the fact her cousin was dead and Robert Carrol was still alive. The cheater didn't deserve to be the one who got to go home every night to his spouse. He didn't deserve to have a spouse in the first place if he was willing to sleep around.

Speaking of his wife, they needed to speak to her. See if she figured out what was going on at the office.

"Fine," Tanner said, releasing Robert.

He immediately straightened his tie and then pulled a tissue from his pocket that he used to wipe his nose. He'd complained of it being broken, but it didn't look like it was. Aimee figured Tanner could have done a whole lot more damage to the man if he'd wanted to. He'd practiced an enormous amount of restraint in her book. But an assault charge wouldn't exactly look good for him considering he was already a suspect for murder.

A buzz sounded as Robert took a seat behind his desk. Tanner stood at the closed door, arms folded over his chest as Aimee took the nearest seat.

"It's the front desk," Robert said. "I need to take this."

"Go ahead," Tanner seethed. "But if you let on anything has happened in here, your nose won't be the only thing I break."

Robert smoothed a hand down his tie and then tapped the phone. "What is it, Cecily?

"The sheriff's deputy is here," Cecily informed. "Says it's urgent and he needs to speak with you."

The front office must be abuzz with all the unusual activity between the two of them being here interrupting the day, BethAnne being gone, and now this.

Robert slid his glance up at Tanner with a look that said the tables had just turned. "Send him back."

They had a matter of seconds to get out of there or be caught by the sheriff's deputy. Aimee had to know if Robert knew about the pregnancy. His reaction would hopefully give her the answer she was searching for. It was now or never.

Aimee looked Robert dead in the eyes. "How long did you know about BethAnne's pregnancy?"

11

"What?" Robert asked, after looking like he was going to have to pick his jaw up off the floor.

Tanner studied the man for any signs he could be lying or covering up. It was a mixed bag. They only had a few seconds before a deputy came walking through the door, so he urged Aimee to stand up.

"I didn't know about a pregnancy," Robert said, still looking very much in shock. Could Tanner believe the bastard? Robert's gaze bounced from Tanner to Aimee and back.

"Help us get out of here without the deputy seeing us, and we won't broadcast the news about the affair," Tanner said, figuring they needed to get out.

Robert pushed up to standing and crossed the room. "Stay here until someone comes for you."

"One last question," Aimee interrupted. "What kind of car do you drive?"

"Range Rover," he supplied. "Why?"

"Never mind," Aimee stated. "It's not that important."

Trusting this man was a risky move but Tanner didn't

see an alternative. He stepped aside so Robert could leave the room. The doctor might be throwing them a curveball. He might come back in a few seconds with the deputy and demand Tanner and Aimee be arrested.

Aimee moved to Tanner's side as he listened at the door. The only thing they could hear was the murmur of voices on the other side. Seconds ticked by that felt like minutes. And then tap-tap-tap, three small raps on the door. It cracked opened and Missy waved for them to come out and follow her.

Robert had the deputy's back to the office. The squawk of the police radio caused his heart to jackhammer his ribs. The law already saw him as a potential suspect. It wouldn't look good for his defense to be here where they were interviewing another suspect. At least, he believed the doctor to be a suspect. It wasn't hard for him and Aimee to find out about the affair that had been going on. The sheriff was the one who'd told Aimee about the pregnancy. But he had also explicitly told her not to interfere with his investigation.

Missy led them through a side door that was most likely the employee entrance and exit.

"Be careful," Missy said to them as she led them outside.

Tanner couldn't help but think she knew something. Since the cat was about to be out of the bag anyway, could he trust Missy with the secret? She was close with BethAnne. Would she have mentioned the pregnancy to Missy? "Did you know who BethAnne was dating?"

Missy's eyebrows drew together in confusion. Her mouth dropped open. "Wasn't she seeing you?"

"No," Tanner said. "We were just friends."

"I know she had a thing for you," Missy explained. Her initial reaction had been too dramatic. Fake?

Yeah, she knew something that she wasn't telling.

Aimee grabbed hold of his arm. "We have to go, Tanner. The deputy can't see us here or we'll both end up in jail, especially you."

Missy glanced around. "The deputy was out here taking pictures of license plates. Just so you know."

Hells bells.

Tanner should have known that would happen. He should have parked further away. Then again, his truck was registered to Firebrand Cattle, so there was no way it could be traced back to him directly.

A jury might not see it that way. And he couldn't count on a fair trial in Lone Star Pass. His mother's case had all but proven the good citizens of their town would be biased. His mother wasn't even safe in jail, not that Tanner couldn't hold his own in any situation. Being ganged up on or taken down by a guard might be a different story. In a fair fight, he didn't doubt himself. But that might not be the case.

"I have to get back before someone notices I'm gone," Missy said, checking behind her like someone might walk up and surprise them.

Aimee nodded. "Thank you for helping us get out of the office. We owe you a huge favor. Maybe a drink?"

"No problem," Missy said. "Don't even worry about it. It's what BethAnne would have wanted."

Tanner led Aimee away from the building and to his truck. He was still kicking himself for parking in the lot, when he should have parked on the street. At least the deputy wouldn't have been able to accuse him of being at the doctor's office.

"Do you think Robert will turn us in?" Aimee asked after he helped her into the truck and then claimed the driver's side.

He started the engine. "Your guess is as good as mine."

He navigated out of the lot and onto the street. "If the deputy asks about the pregnancy or if Robert thinks they suspect the affair, he might turn me in to deflect attention away from himself."

"I feared as much," she said. "I'll testify that you had nothing to do with this."

"Robert says he was fishing two days ago," Tanner said, shifting the topic. He didn't want to consider the fact anyone might have to step forward to protect him. "I was working the land by myself like usual."

"I'm sure someone saw you," Aimee pointed out.

"I spend hours out on the land doing my own thing," he said. "Ranching is a terrible alibi, when most of our work is alone. It would be easy to hide behind."

"But fishing?" Aimee drummed her fingers on the armrest. "Seriously? Would anyone believe the silk tie-wearing doctor was really fishing by himself?"

"If he was cheating with BethAnne, there's no telling who else he might be sleeping with at the office," Tanner pointed out.

"Missy?"

"We probably shouldn't rule her out," he realized. Something was niggling at the back of his mind that he couldn't quite put his finger on about the billing clerk. "How close was BethAnne with Missy?"

"Good question," Aimee said. "I know the two went out for Mexican food and margaritas after work on Fridays sometimes."

"BethAnne mentioned her co-worker to me a few times, but I used to tune out when she started talking about work." What he wouldn't give to hear his friend's endless chatter about all matters, including all that went on at her job. Hell, he'd give his right arm to have a few more days with Beth-

Anne. She'd been a good friend. And the one who'd told him about Alicia's fake pregnancy, so he could let his brother Rowan know the person he trusted in a relationship had lied to him big time. Lying about a child to get a marriage proposal out of someone had to be the lowest low. BethAnne had broken protocol to tell him so that Rowan could rest easy after his girlfriend dropped the bomb and then disappeared when his brother asked for a paternity test.

Tanner hated secrets.

"Where to next?" Aimee asked.

"Didn't you tell the sheriff we would stop by in a little while?" he asked, figuring he was going to have to face the music of questioning at some point. He had nothing to hide but recent experience with the law didn't give him a whole lot of confidence in the system.

Plus, the thing niggling at the back of his mind became more and more persistent. What was it trying to tell him?

"Yes, but I think that's a mistake under the circumstances," Aimee pointed out. "You don't have a solid alibi for the time period during BethAnne's murder and could end up arrested if we're not careful. I won't get as far without you if you're locked behind bars."

"I'll do my best to make certain that doesn't happen," he said. "But I'm afraid I can't make any promises."

"I know. I don't expect you to either." She reached over and touched his arm. Contact sent electricity rocketing up his arm. He'd thought about the kiss they'd shared more than he wanted to admit. But this wasn't the time.

And then it dawned on him what had been bothering him about Missy. "She didn't tell us to say hello to BethAnne for her one time while we were at the office."

"Who didn't?"

"Missy," he confirmed. "If she thought BethAnne was at home not feeling well, wouldn't she tell us to say hello or give her a message?"

"Normally, yes," she admitted as her eyes widened.

And then he realized something else.

"She said, 'was,' when she was talking about BethAnne," he continued. "Remember? She said, 'because she *was* most definitely not an outdoorsy girl.'"

Aimee brought a hand up to cover her gasp.

~

Aimee released a string of swear words low and under her breath. Tanner was right. Something had struck her as odd too, but she couldn't quite put her finger on it until now. "I believe so."

"She knows more than she's willing to let on," he stated, clearly thinking out loud.

Could Missy have known about the office affair? If Beth-Anne hadn't told her own cousin, would she tell a friend from work she wasn't as close to? "Robert drives a Range Rover."

"I'm glad you asked the question." Tanner turned onto the road that she was sure led to the sheriff's office. "I meant to."

"We need to speak to his wife either way," Aimee pointed out. "I'm still not certain whether or not I believe Robert about being out fishing. If there are others he was sleeping with, we need to talk to them. They need to be made aware they aren't his only one."

"I agree," Tanner said. "People need all the facts so they can make an informed decision about what they want to do in the future. As awful as it sounds, they need to know when they're being played too."

"I suspect that's what is happening with Robert," she reasoned. It made sense the man wouldn't stop with one. "I highly doubt he had true feelings for BethAnne. Based on our conversation, he seemed more like he was taking advantage of her loneliness."

"Which is a jerk move," he said.

"There are all kinds of people out there, Tanner."

He knew better than anyone. "You think you know someone and then find out they were only showing you one side of themselves."

"I just wish I knew why BethAnne didn't trust me enough to tell me what was going on," Aimee said. "I feel like I let her down."

"It's understandable but none of this is your fault." He didn't point out the obvious that BethAnne was dead because of *her secrets* and not anything Aimee said, did, or didn't do, and she appreciated him for it.

"It's weird how guilt works, isn't it?"

He nodded and tightened his grip on the steering wheel. She remembered him talking about his mother's situation— a situation BethAnne had been distressed over as well. He, of all people, could probably relate to everything she just said on more than one level.

"There's been plenty of it to go around," he said so quietly she almost didn't hear him. After issuing a sharp sigh, he said, "I should probably call the family lawyer before I head inside the sheriff's office."

"Seems like a good idea." When did life spin so far out of control? The idea Tanner Firebrand, a person she'd only ever known to be decent and upstanding, honest to a fault, could be held on murder charges was so foreign to her that she could scarcely believe this was reality. The fact BethAnne would never send an inappropriate but funny joke text again didn't seem like it could be real. And the notion Aimee would never meet BethAnne for chips, salsa, and margaritas again made her plain sad.

Denial was lessening, though. And reality was setting in. Going back to BethAnne's house, Aimee didn't expect her cousin's car to be there now. It was a start. The thought of seeing her aunt and uncle at the sheriff's office was both comforting and emotional.

Tanner turned into the parking lot of the sheriff's office, pulled up to a front spot, and parked. He cut the engine off. In the next second, he was exiting the truck.

"Whoa, hold on," Aimee started. "Shouldn't you make that call to the lawyer?"

"After I thought about it, I decided against it." He closed the door and then rounded the front of the vehicle to open the passenger door. "Do you know what a guilty person does when being questioned by the law?"

"Brings in his or her lawyer?"

"Exactly," he confirmed. "I have nothing to hide, even though I was on the land without any witnesses after our morning meeting in the barn. The evidence will prove that I'm innocent because I am."

"Robert has much more to lose if word about the pregnancy gets out," Aimee stated. "He will jump to the top of the suspect list."

"As he should," Tanner pointed out. "I'm still on the fence as to whether or not he is responsible for BethAnne's murder. Not to mention the fact Missy knows something that she's not speaking up about."

"Maybe she's too scared." A co-worker turning up dead

with their mouth sewn shut is a powerful warning against talking.

"The method of death was no doubt meant to send a message," he agreed. "We realized that the minute we saw BethAnne."

"Burying someone in a shallow grave, essentially dumping the body and hoping to get away with murder, makes me think the person didn't care one bit about my cousin." Aimee couldn't imagine doing that to another human being, let alone someone she'd been in a relationship with. Then again, she didn't think like a killer.

"Everything happened fast," he said. "That was the reason for the shallow grave." He was onto something. "The person felt the need to move quickly, which means BethAnne was likely about to expose someone."

"Like a whistleblower?" Aimee asked.

"Could be," he confirmed. "I'm just thinking out loud here, trying to make sense of a senseless act."

Aimee touched Tanner's arm. He turned to her and pulled her into an embrace. He held her so tenderly, for a moment, she felt safe. She relaxed into him and borrowed from his strength.

He must have needed the moment just as much as she did. He touched his forehead to hers, closed his eyes, and took in a deep breath.

A moment later, he stepped back, looked her in the eyes, and asked, "Ready?"

She smiled and nodded, trying to stay positive if only to offer some reassurance.

Would he be arrested? Or would they get answers?

12

The two-story building was nondescript, brown bricks with tall, thin windows. Tanner and Aimee were almost immediately checked in and walked down the hallway to the sheriff's office. Tanner tried not to take the speed with which they were escorted as a bad sign. The gray clouds already cast a dark shadow over the day. And it had been one helluva long twelve hours. His stomach reminded him they hadn't eaten, but he could ignore hunger. Food was sometimes a luxury while hunting poachers and he could make do with very little despite his size and usual appetite.

Lawler stood up and came around his desk the minute he saw them in the doorway. He'd been given a heads up they were headed his way. His face muscles were tense and he had a cup of coffee in his hand.

"Coffee?" he asked, holding up his cup.

"That'd be nice," Tanner responded after Aimee said yes.

Lawler nodded toward his deputy, who disappeared down the hallway. Then, he turned his full attention on the two of them. "Have a seat, please." He motioned toward the chairs opposite his desk.

Aimee picked the seat closest to the wall, leaving the one next to the door open for Tanner. He took his place and the sheriff sat down. He set down the coffee cup and clasped his hands together.

"I have a problem," he started.

Tanner leaned forward, resting his elbows on his knees. "What is that, Sheriff?" Or, maybe more importantly, what could they do to help solve it?

"The rope used in Ms. Dyer's murder is consistent with the kind of rope used at Firebrand Cattle," he explained.

"How is that a problem?" Tanner asked. "Most of the county buys rope from the exact same supplier."

"That's true," Lawler agreed. "And it's only one data point. Usually in an investigation, multiple data points line up to point to a suspect."

"Go on," Tanner urged, thinking he might need to bring in Harlen Sawyer after all. The family attorney went way back with Tanner's grandfather and would be able to find the right defense lawyer, if it came to that. Then again, his soon-to-be sister-in-law Tara Dowling had good references. She'd brought in the best criminal lawyer to defend Tanner's mother.

Hell. When did he have to start thinking about defending himself against a murder charge? The whole idea was surreal. But he also realized dragging his heels in denial would hurt him more than help, so he wouldn't take any of this lightly. If it could happen to him, it could happen to anybody.

"You were friends with BethAnne," the sheriff continued.

"Yes," he confirmed. "I think that's common knowledge at this point."

"How close were the two of you?" Sheriff Lawler asked.

"Not close enough to be anything but friends," he defended. "And not the kind with 'benefits' if that's where you're headed with this."

"Are you saying that you're not the father of Ms. Dyer's baby?" Lawler asked.

"That's correct," Tanner said as Aimee listened quietly. "I'm sure you can take a DNA sample to prove it. I'm willing to do just that, if it'll move this investigation along so you can focus on the actual killer instead of continuing to bark up the wrong tree." His voice got a little heated at the end of his sentence because the sheriff *was* barking up the wrong tree, and it *was* costing the investigation valuable time. The longer this case went unsolved, the colder the trail would become. He'd learned a few things about how these things work in recent months since members of his family had been drawn into legal cases.

At this point, he was beginning to think the family was cursed ever since the Marshall's death. It would be just like his grandfather to put some kind of hex on his descendants. Granted, there were reasons for his behavior that Tanner understood but still couldn't forgive.

And the man's legacy was having one of his grandchildren suspected of murder. *Thanks a helluva lot.*

"I appreciate your willingness to cooperate," the sheriff said before jotting down a note on the pad of paper in front of him. "I'd like someone from the lab to take a swab before you leave here tonight."

"Done," Tanner said. "Call whoever you need to and make the arrangements. Let's settle this distraction now, so we can all move on." He did realize this might not put him completely in the clear, but it would go a long way toward proving his innocence.

The fact he had to prove he didn't murder one of his friends in cold blood in the first place sent white-hot anger roaring through him.

"What else?" he asked, hearing the curtness in his tone.

Sheriff Lawler held up a finger before using it to press an intercom button on his phone. "Can we bring in the representative from BioIdentity Lab? Mr. Firebrand is willing to cooperate with a DNA test."

Aimee reached over and placed her hand in his. He gave a gentle squeeze for reassurance. This would be alright. It had to be.

Once the sheriff finished the intercom conversation, he clasped his hands together again and set them on top of his desk. "What were you both doing at Dr. Carrol's office a little while ago?"

The deputy had taken pictures of vehicles in the parking lot, so denying they were there would do no good. Plus, it would make the sheriff even more suspicious once he found out they were lying.

"Tanner drove me to pick up a few of my cousin's personal effects," Aimee spoke up. "I'm afraid it's my fault we were there."

"Why did you feel the need to go to your cousin's workplace now?" Sheriff Lawler asked.

"I'm not sure how long I'll be in town and part of me wanted to close that loop as soon as possible," Aimee admitted. The absence of her 'tell' signs meant she was telling a partial truth at the very least. It also meant she believed what she was saying, which was more important anyway. She was far more convincing that way.

Plus, he liked the fact she was a bad liar. Folks shouldn't get too comfortable deceiving others.

"It's understandable," the sheriff conceded.

"Also, just a quick question," she continued.

"Please, go ahead," Sheriff Lawler urged. Some of the tension lines in his face eased, which Tanner took as a good sign. It was too early to be relieved, but it was a start in the right direction at the very least. He'd take what he could get under the circumstances.

"Are my aunt and uncle still here?" she asked. "I saw their SUV in the parking lot but, obviously, I haven't seen them since we got here."

"Yes," Sheriff Lawler said as the deputy stepped into the doorway holding two cups of coffee. A look exchanged between sheriff and deputy that Tanner took as another good sign. "Would you like to see them?"

"That would be nice," Aimee said before turning to Tanner. "Unless you need me here, in which case I'll stay."

"Go," Tanner said. "They need to see you too."

"I'll be back in a few minutes," Aimee promised.

"It'll give us enough time to put this DNA business behind us," Tanner stated, hoping it was true.

The deputy handed over the coffees. "I can take you down the hall to the witness room where they're waiting, Ms. Anderson."

Aimee stepped around Tanner as someone wearing a white lab coat eased past the deputy into the room. She held a small kit that looked like something that would come with a science experiment kit.

Tanner took a deep breath. Despite knowing full well there wasn't a chance in hell he was the father of BethAnne's child, nerves settled over him. "How long does it take to get the results?"

The sheriff looked to the short, perky brunette with long tight curls wearing the lab coat.

"I can have preliminary results in twenty minutes," she practically chirped, clearly proud of herself. "Of course, we'll want to send out the samples to verify. That will take at least twenty-four hours to get a result. But the rapid test works much like a strep test at the doctor's office. The results have a high-reliability rating."

Not exactly the comfort he was looking for when it came to being arrested for murder, but the results should confirm there's no chance he would have been the father.

In roughly twenty minutes, the sheriff could move on to more fruitful suspects, like Dr. Carrol, for instance. Telling the sheriff would bust Aimee for interfering with the investigation, and potentially get her into a heap of trouble. Tanner couldn't do that to her. Or himself. He was just as guilty. The motive would speak for itself. The sheriff was smart and capable. The investigation would lead him to the doctor.

～

The minute Aunt Denise saw Aimee in the doorway, her sobs echoed. She immediately stood up and made a beeline for Aimee before wrapping her in a good Southern hug. "Oh, baby, what have they done to our girl? They took her from us."

"I know, Aunt Denise," Aimee soothed. "I'm so sorry." She said other words, like this wasn't fair and BethAnne didn't deserve to have this happen to her but they felt hollow in the face of the horrific act and the loss that would never be replaced. Throwing the bastard in jail for life might bring a sense of justice but it couldn't bring BethAnne back.

Uncle Chuckie joined them, wrapping his big bear-like arms around them in a huddle type of hug. "You were a good friend to our Bethie. She couldn't have asked for a better cousin or best friend."

"I just wish she'd told me more," she admitted, allowing tears to drop that had been welling in her eyes. She no longer had the energy to fight them while being wrapped in the love of her aunt and uncle. "Maybe there was something I could have done to help or stop this from happening."

"Don't you do that to yourself," her aunt scolded. "It was our job to protect her, not yours. You hear me?"

"She loved you guys more than words," Aimee said to them. They should know how much their daughter loved them. They deserved to know they were amazing parents, unlike Aimee's who'd left her to her own defenses most of her childhood.

She couldn't be certain how long they stood there, hugging and reassuring each other. Five minutes? Ten?

Uncle Chuckie broke the circle first and then Aunt Denise followed.

"The sheriff is being stingy with information," Aunt Denise said, motioning toward the chairs they'd been sitting in before Aimee showed up.

She took a seat beside her aunt, who was in the middle. How much should she tell them about what they'd learned so far? "What did he say?"

"That you'd identified..." Aunt Denise choked up. "You'd been the one to confirm it was our Bethie."

"I was," Aimee said.

"That must have been a terrible thing to witness," Aunt Denise said. She was the talker of the family. Uncle Chuckie had always been the steady, quiet one.

"It was," she confirmed without going into further detail

about the conditions. "A whole mess of folks showed up to help search. BethAnne was loved in this community." She hoped those words could bring a tiny bit of solace to her aunt and uncle.

Uncle Chuckie nodded his appreciation. He looked old and tired, more so than she'd ever seen.

"One of the Firebrand men came up on the..." She flashed eyes at them, unable to finish. "The search had been called off due to weather but a few of us decided to stay and keep searching."

"We'll have to send a card to the Firebrands," Aunt Denise said. She was the rare person who still sent handwritten notes to people to thank them or during the holidays. Getting those cards in the mail had reminded Aimee of a bygone time, now that everyone communicated via group chat, text, or e-mails. People rarely made phone calls anymore, so letter writing was definitely a lost art. Those cards and letters were gold.

Aimee thought about the test that was going on in the other room. Tanner wasn't the father. But there was always the worry of a faulty test. She'd learned not to trust anything or anyone over the years.

The sheriff had no reason to set Tanner up for murder, despite the turmoil and accusations going on in the Firebrand family right now after Jackie Firebrand's arrest. The town might be ready to convict a Firebrand without adequate proof, but the sheriff seemed like a good lawman. He seemed good at his job and a thorough investigator.

She understood him needing to question all friends of BethAnne who would have access to a rope and be strong enough to pull off strangling her and then dragging her body into the grave where she'd been buried. But she wouldn't rest easy until the correct test results came in.

"What has the sheriff told you so far?" Aunt Denise asked, wiping away her tears and then sitting up straighter.

Aimee needed to stall because she wouldn't lie to her relatives, but the sheriff didn't want details getting out just yet.

"What you said so far," Aimee said. "He isn't wanting to talk too much about his investigation, which is understandable under the circumstances."

"How did it happen?" Aunt Denise asked. "Did he tell you that much at least?"

Aimee opened her mouth to speak and then clamped it shut when Tanner appeared at the door. "Aunt Denise, you've met Tanner Firebrand."

"Of course, I have but it's been years since we've had a conversation," Aunt Denise admitted.

Tanner squeezed into the small room and offered his condolences. He shook Uncle Chuckie's hand and then Aunt Denise's.

And then he set his eyes on Aimee. "Do you have a minute to speak in the hallway?"

Her heart dropped as fear of the worst enveloped her.

13

"I'll be right back," Aimee said to her relatives before ducking into the hallway. Tanner had seen pictures of BethAnne's parents and probably had seen her mother during their school days, what felt like a hundred years ago. He didn't spend much time in town, preferring to head to Austin or Houston if he wanted to go out and meet people. A lot of young folks moved away to go to college and then headed to one of the bigger cities to work after graduation. Only a handful stayed back to help with family businesses, so the dating pool shrank considerably over the years.

A look of panic crossed Aimee's features once the door was closed. "Everything turn out okay?"

"Yes, good," he confirmed, finally exhaling.

She pushed up to her tiptoes and looped her arms around his neck. "I knew it would be fine but my imagination ran wild."

"Mine too," he admitted, wrapping his arms around her waist. She felt a little too right in his arms and he breathed a little too easily when their bodies were in contact. "Strange how the mind works sometimes."

"I don't want to do this without you," she whispered. Aimee was strong. She would be fine with or without him. And yet, all his protective instincts flared. He wanted to keep her safe even though he knew, logically, she didn't need his help.

"I'm here," he reassured.

"Did you tell the sheriff about the affair?" she asked.

"No," he admitted. "I figured the sheriff would make the discovery on his own and I didn't want him to know we stopped by and questioned the doctor before the deputy arrived. Lawler might see that as us interfering. The deputy should have asked Dr. Carrol if he knew of BethAnne being in a relationship with anyone. The hope is that her boss will come clean. Otherwise, they'll figure it out when they canvass neighbors."

"Mrs. Weller will speak her mind and tell them about Dr. Carrol's frequent after-work visits across the street," she said. "Do you think text or phone records will give away the affair?"

"It's possible. But my guess is the doctor would be smart enough not to leave a trail," he reasoned. "Plus, they worked together so it would be easy enough for him to tell her when he was free to stop by."

Aimee bit her bottom lip as she looked up at him. "I'd still like to speak to Mrs. Carrol just to see if she figured it out."

"Agreed," he said. "Plus, I'd like to get Missy out of the office and talk to her for five minutes. She was holding something back and I have a feeling she might be more inclined to open up away from work."

"It wouldn't be hard to find out where she lives."

"We could swing by on our way out of here," he said. "Unless you'd rather go home and get a few hours of sleep, in which case we could be waiting at her car as she leaves for work tomorrow morning."

"I doubt I could get any sleep to be honest," she admitted. "I'm beyond wired."

He nodded. "We're missing an important puzzle piece somewhere."

"It has to be the muscle car, right?"

"I've been thinking along those same lines," he said. "Maybe it will lead us to some answers at the very least."

"I feel like we've hit a wall with our investigation, Tanner."

"Walls were meant to be pushed through," he encouraged. "We'll keep going until we find the answers we're looking for. It's what BethAnne deserves."

"I know how much you cared about my cousin," Aimee said. "She might have wished there was more, but your friendship as it was meant the world to her."

"That means more than you know." He meant it too. A thought crossed his mind. "We should track down Alicia while we're at it. See what kind of car she drives or has access to."

Aimee cocked her head to one side and her eyebrows drew together. "Would she be strong enough to pull something like this off?"

"I'm thinking she might have enlisted a relative," he said. "It might be far-fetched but at this point I'd rather not rule anything out. Alicia would have an axe to grind with BethAnne for letting the cat out of the bag to me about the nonpregnancy."

"Tricking someone into marriage versus actually killing another human being is a big leap," Aimee surmised.

"I know," he admitted. "And it might be grasping at straws, but any trail is worth following up on at this point. Believe me when I say women are capable of attempting murder or being vindictive enough to arrange murder. If Alicia believed BethAnne ruined her life, she might be out for revenge. Sewing her mouth closed would make sense not as a warning to someone else but as a punishment."

Aimee issued a sharp sigh. "You're right. We can't afford to rule anyone out. Plus, just because Dr. Carrol might have fathered BethAnne's child doesn't mean he would have killed her to get rid of the baby. I'd think he might actually think twice about destroying two lives."

The sheriff stepped into the hallway and motioned for them to join him at the other end. Tanner released his hold on Aimee as the two of them turned to make the dozen or so steps to reach Lawler.

"I just got a phone call from the coroner." He paused for a beat. "The pregnancy was going to abort itself. He said it's not uncommon for a first pregnancy not to make it to the three-month mark."

This could explain why BethAnne hadn't informed Dr. Carrol of the pregnancy. If she realized there wasn't a viable fetus, there wasn't anything to tell and most folks knew enough to wait until the three month mark to tell anyone. Even he knew that was common.

"Makes sense," Aimee said. Based on her tone, she'd picked up on the same thing he was thinking.

"Which also means she might not have mentioned the pregnancy to the father," Sheriff Lawler said.

"I'm guessing this shifts the investigation away from the person she was secretly dating," Aimee continued.

"We can't rule this person out," Lawler said. "There could have been a reason she kept his identity a secret."

"Until now, I thought my cousin told me everything."

"Working in my business, nothing surprises me anymore," the sheriff admitted with a look of compassion.

"Does this mean we can keep the pregnancy news under wraps?" Aimee asked. "My aunt and uncle have no idea as far as I can tell and I'd like to keep it that way if at all possible. They're already going through enough grief without piling it on."

"I have no reason to discuss this aspect of the case with anyone," the sheriff said.

"Thank you, Sheriff. It means a lot."

"I know you want to protect your relatives," the lawman said. "I'd want to do the same if I was in your position. Plus, there's no reason to inform them."

"Inform us of what?" Aunt Denise said from down the hall. She stood there with her hands on her hips. Tanner figured all hell was about to break loose based on the older woman's expression.

∼

AIMEE MADE a beeline toward her aunt. "It's not something you want to know, Aunt Denise. Believe me."

She ushered her relatives back into the witness room.

Aunt Denise made a show of staring Aimee down. Her aunt could be intimidating when she wanted to be. "Are you sure about that?"

"Would I lie to you?" Aimee could argue she'd lied by omission, by not telling them about the pregnancy, but BethAnne wouldn't have wanted her parents to know or she would have told them herself. In fact, the sheriff found out due to the autopsy and not because there was any communication about the situation.

"No, I guess not," Aunt Denise conceded.

Uncle Chuckie followed suit with whatever his wife wanted, reciting the old saying *a happy wife equals a happy life*. But the same could apply to any kind of partner when she really thought about it.

"I think it's best the less you know about the case, Aunt Denise." She looked first at her aunt and then at her uncle. "What happened isn't good and the sheriff is doing his best to keep the details away from the public. One, to honor BethAnne. And the other reason has to do with the nature of how she was found. Believe me when I say that you'll sleep a lot better at night if you don't know. Knowing won't bring her back and it'll only cause you more misery than you deserve."

Aunt Denise stood with her hands on her hips. She tensed like she was getting ready to take a punch after the last bit of information. And then she exhaled. Her shoulders sagged forward. "You're probably right, hon. There's a part of me that wants to know and the other part says it'll only break my heart worse."

"The most important thing moving forward is finding the person responsible for taking BethAnne away from us," Aimee noted.

"You're right, hon."

"Why don't you head home and try to get some rest," Aimee said. Her aunt had severe bags underneath her eyes and looked exhausted. "Staying here won't do any good for either one of you. You'll be more comfortable at home, and I promise to call with any news should there be any."

Aunt Denise stood there for a long moment, staring at the wall behind Aimee. "I guess you're right, hon. We should head on home." She threw her arms in the air. "We aren't doing anything here other than breathing."

Aimee brought her aunt into a hug.

"I love you, hon." Those were foreign words to Aimee. She couldn't remember the last time she heard either one of her parents utter them. Her parents divorced when she was young, and she hadn't seen him since kindergarten.

"You too," was the best she could muster. It wasn't nearly enough but it was all she had to give.

Uncle Chuckie was next. He brought her into one of his bear hugs. "Be careful."

"I will," she promised. "Plus, I have Tanner to watch my back."

Her uncle gave a nod of approval.

"I'm staying at BethAnne's while I'm in town," Aimee said. "We'll have to figure out what we want to do with her house and her personal things."

"I can swing by tomorrow to get started," her aunt said.

"Let's give it a couple of days in case the sheriff's office wants to look around inside, okay?"

"That's probably a good idea," Aunt Denise said with another sniffle. "Let me know when it's a good day."

Aimee would never be ready to close up her cousin's home, but the daunting task would have to be faced at some point in the near future. "I will."

"Alright then, we'll be on our way," Aunt Denise said, looking about as lost as a person could be. Uncle Chuckie was in the same boat.

"Drive safe," Aimee said as they walked toward the lobby.

Aunt Denise waved a hand behind her back in acknowledgment. Watching them walk away was hard.

She met Tanner and the sheriff at the end of the hallway. "Is there any reason for us to be here?"

"I guess not," Sheriff Lawler said. He turned to Tanner. "Your willingness to cooperate is much appreciated."

Tanner nodded. "I have no reason to hold up this investigation. As a matter of fact, I want nothing more than to narrow down the suspect list so the person responsible can be caught. If submitting to a DNA test takes me off the suspect list, so be it."

The sheriff dropped his gaze to the floor. "You're classified as a witness for the time being."

"I have no plans to be reclassified," he quipped before turning to Aimee. "Are you ready to head out?"

"Yes." She turned toward the sheriff. "You'll call me the minute you have news if anything changes?"

"You can count on it," the sheriff said.

Tanner reached for her hand and then linked their fingers before walking down the hall, through the lobby, and out the door.

"It's unbelievable that I could still be considered a suspect," he said to Aimee after they claimed their seats in the truck.

"I couldn't agree more," she replied.

"Right now, all we have is the doctor, Missy, and the muscle car to go on," he said as he navigated onto the street. "What are we missing?"

"The pregnancy turned out to be a non-issue, right?"

"It's probably safe to assume BethAnne kept it a secret from everyone, including the father," he agreed while making a right turn.

He glanced in the rearview mirror and then made a face.

"Everything alright?" she asked, glancing back to find a pair of headlights half a street back.

"I'm not sure," he said before making a sharp left. He

watched the rearview as the pair of headlights came around the corner.

"Is someone following us?" she asked.

Tanner white-knuckled the steering wheel. "There's only one way to find out."

14

There were no streetlights on this stretch of roadway. It was too dark to get a good look at the vehicle behind them. Tanner cut the wheel right, making a last-minute turn. The car, which was half a block behind, followed.

What were the chances the only other car on the street happened to be making the same turns? A set of headlights flashed.

"What does that mean?" Aimee asked as she craned her neck around to get a better view behind them.

He glanced up at the rearview. "Let's see how determined they are to get to us. Hold tight, okay? I'm going to see if I can lose this jerk. Stay low, just in case they start shooting, since we don't know what we're dealing with yet."

"Will do," she reassured as he mashed the gas pedal and pushed the engine. It was late and he was driving on a residential street. The engine noise might bring out some of the residents. Witnesses might not be the worst thing in this situation. These days, someone always had a camera phone on the ready to record every incident, big and small, for the world to see on social media.

Privacy didn't exist anymore. In this case, it might benefit him so he wouldn't hop on his soapbox about how folks should be able to walk out in public without the possibility of ending up on someone's social media account for the world to see. Ever since his mother's arrest, his side of the family had been living under a microscope. Living in a fishbowl in recent weeks had been the worst.

Being a Firebrand had already placed a spotlight on him. It was part of the reason he loved being out on the land so much. No spotlight there. Out there, even Wi-Fi wasn't guaranteed. Some of his best days had been spent with no bars on his phone.

The herd didn't care one way or another about the internet. There was something comforting and familiar about working cattle. Ranching was the last frontier, a simple life that wasn't for everyone.

Dating was a different story, not that he was looking to settle down. How could he when his mother was up on attempted murder charges?

The car behind them kept pace and enough distance so that he couldn't see who was in the driver's seat. There could be more than one person in the car. Someone could be hunkered down in the passenger seat with a weapon on the ready.

Of course, the driver had no idea whether or not Tanner and Aimee were stocked with weapons and ammunition. Most country folks carried a shotgun in their trucks at the very least since many were hunters. The almost nonexistent crime rate, until recent months anyway, ensured shotguns were safe inside vehicles.

Up ahead, there was a fork in the road. He set his blinker

toward turning right. The car behind him kept distance, so there was no way he could lose them at the last minute.

Tanner cut left. The vehicle followed.

"The driver isn't pushing the speed," he noticed. "They aren't trying to run up alongside us either."

Aimee shook her head. "They're not ramming up against the bumper or getting close enough for us to see who is inside."

"Or trying to run us off the road," he pointed out. "My question at this point is, what makes them think we won't call in the law?"

"I was just wondering the same thing," she said. "We can't tell who they are, but one thing is certain, we would have heard the engine if this was a muscle car."

"Exactly," he agreed. "And this might be someone who knows we don't want the law involved any more than they do."

Stopping to find out what they wanted meant risking Aimee's life. It wasn't a risk he could take lightly.

"What does this person want?" she asked again.

"Good question. We'll have to pull over to find out."

"Is that a good idea?"

"No," he confirmed. "But what choice do we have?"

"It might be safer if we stop and let them come to us," she reasoned. "Rather than go to them where they could open fire."

"Being here with the engine running could give us a head start if this thing goes south," he agreed.

"Let's go for it," she said with a whole mess of trepidation in her voice. It was a risky move but doing nothing didn't seem like the right play either.

Tanner slowed to a stop as he pulled over on the residential street, idling the engine. There were no porchlights on, which cast the street in darkness other than two pairs of headlights.

The driver behind kept theirs on what felt like high beams. The lights flickered again. Tanner shook his head. He rolled down his window and then waved for the driver to come to them. There was no way he was leaving Aimee alone in the truck or the driver's seat for that matter. They would be safer staying put, which was what he intended to do.

For what felt like an eternity, but really must have only been a couple of minutes, they were at a standstill. Tanner held his ground. He also discreetly reached underneath the seat to retrieve the .45 Colt he kept there for emergency use. The weapon was handy to keep around when he was out on the land when a wild boar or coyote came around. Both were menaces to the herd and had to be dealt with on sight or things could get out of hand fast.

The driver's side door opened.

"Looks like they made up their mind," he whispered. "Be ready for anything."

A female emerged and walked toward the driver's side. As she came closer into view, Tanner realized who the mystery person was.

Missy?

"Why on earth would she be following us?" Aimee said.

"Be on the lookout," he warned. "If she so much as reaches into her purse for a tube of lipstick, assume the worst. Expect her to pull out a gun and start firing."

"Okay," Aimee said.

"My foot is hovering over the gas pedal." He handed over the Colt. "Do you know how to shoot?"

"Yes," she admitted, taking the offering.

"Keep the barrel low," he instructed. "We don't want to spook her either."

The thought of battling it out here on the street in a residential neighborhood didn't appeal to him in the least. Being exposed wasn't exactly a good feeling either. But what choice did they have?

The car was determined to follow them. There'd been something in Missy's eyes at the office that had sent up red flags about her. Did she know something? Or did she do something? Either way, they were about to find out.

~

Aimee's hand trembled as she held the .45 Colt. She'd shot at cans at various distances, but that was a whole different story than shooting a human being at point-blank range. Not to mention the fact Tanner was in between her and the potential target.

Not exactly ideal conditions.

Then there was the window to consider. It was a smaller opening than she'd like. Adrenaline had her hand shaking so she couldn't be certain about the accuracy of her shot. Miss by a few inches and Tanner might be picking shrapnel out of his chest.

Deep breaths.

Missy appeared at the driver's side window, looking wide-eyed and disheveled like a crack dealer, unsure if they were walking up to sell drugs to a cop.

Aimee placed her handbag over the weapon.

"I couldn't speak openly at the office," Missy said as her wild gaze scanned the inside of the truck. Was she looking for a gun? She must realize Tanner would have one inside since it wasn't uncommon for ranchers to carry.

"This is a strange way to go about flagging us down," Tanner said. "Keep your hands where we can see 'em."

"Oh, right, I guess not," she said as she raised her hands and then placed them over the open window. "I should have known better than to walk up to the truck without showing my hands. I've just never been in a situation like this before. And, honestly, don't ever want to be again, if you know what I mean."

"What situation?" Tanner asked.

Missy made eyes at them both. "You know. *This*. It's just that BethAnne and I were more than co-workers. We were friends. She was pretty much the only friend I've ever had, you know? She cared about people." Missy sighed. "I remember this one time I was sick, and Dr. Carrol threatened to fire me if I didn't get my butt back to work. BethAnne pulled double duty to make sure the billing stayed up to date while I recovered. I was so sick I couldn't stand up, and she brought me homemade soup and checked on me throughout the day."

This walk down Memory Lane was heartwarming but Aimee wasn't seeing the point of it just yet. Yes, BethAnne was a sweet person. More than sweet, she was kind. She was also genuine and trustworthy.

"My cousin was the best kind of person and friend," Aimee spoke up, hoping this conversation could move along. Especially since Missy seemed more paranoid as time ticked on, scanning the street behind them and checking houses.

"What are you afraid of?" Aimee asked.

"You know how it is nowadays," Missy informed. "You never know who is watching anymore between all those Ring cameras on people's doors and camera phones. Someone could be recording us right now."

Aimee wished she'd thought about doing just that before Missy had walked up to the truck actually. Calling 911 hadn't been an option since they'd had no idea what they were dealing with and there hadn't been an actual threat to either one of them. An operator wouldn't take them seriously if they said they thought a car was following them.

Law enforcement had bigger fish to fry with a murder investigation on their plate, and Aimee and Tanner had just left the sheriff's office.

Back at the office, she'd been certain Missy was hiding something. It was time to come clean.

"BethAnne really was the best," Missy continued. "Which is why she didn't deserve to die."

"How did you know about the murder?" Tanner asked.

Missy's face twisted in shock and confusion. "She didn't show up for work or call. She didn't answer any of my texts asking where she was." She paused and looked at them like the answer had been as plain as the nose on her face.

"Did you know about BethAnne and Dr. Carrol?" Aimee asked.

"They thought they were hiding the affair, but it was common knowledge at the office," Missy admitted. "Sheila was especially offended by it."

"Who is Sheila?" Tanner asked before Aimee could.

"You don't know Sheila?" Missy looked surprised. "Oh, right. I guess you wouldn't know her. She's a lab tech who comes in and out. Likes to pick up samples personally and spend time in Dr. Carrol's office, but that stopped once he started seeing BethAnne."

"Who knew about these affairs?" Tanner asked with disdain.

"I say it was common knowledge, but in truth I was one of the only people who could confirm it," Missy said. "To the others, it was all rumor mill and gossip. Sheila, on the other hand, must have been angry because he stopped closing the door when she came to pick up lab work and their 'work' lunches stopped."

"Isn't Dr. Carrol married?" Tanner asked.

"Yes, as a matter of fact, he is," Missy said. "Doesn't seem to slow him down or stop him, though."

"He made it seem like BethAnne was the only person he'd been having an affair with," Aimee said.

"I bet he did," Missy said, puckering her mouth in disgust like she'd just eaten a pickled prune. "But he goes from one bed to the next. BethAnne didn't seem to realize it, though. He told her that he loved her when I confronted her about it. She said he denied ever having a relationship with Sheila when I pointed that out too."

"What about his wife?" Aimee asked. "BethAnne wasn't the type to sleep with a married man." It occurred to Aimee that might be the reason BethAnne never mentioned the affair to her. Maybe she was waiting until they were official. Then again, a serial cheater had to have all this down pat.

"No, she wasn't," Missy said with a look. "Julia isn't the type to go down without a fight either. She's all about appearances too. Rumor has it that her family put Dr. Carrol through medical school after the two met in college. Julia comes from Houston oil money from way back in the day."

"Seems odd someone like her would want to move to a small town like Lone Star Pass," Tanner pointed out.

"She's back and forth from what I understand," Missy said. "Dr. Carrol uses that to gain sympathy if you ask me."

"Is Julia in town now?" Tanner asked.

"I have no idea," Missy said. "As much as she comes and goes, who knows? I'm certain that she tries to keep her husband on a short leash, though."

"How so?" Aimee asked.

"Cameras at their home," Missy said. "She tracks him with one of those apps on the phone. I overheard him explaining why he'd been at the gym for three hours once."

"She doesn't sound like the kind of person who likes to lose," Tanner said.

"No, she isn't," Missy agreed.

A porchlight came on. A look of panic crossed Missy's features.

15

"I have to go," Missy said before Tanner could stop her. Her face turned sheet-white, like she'd seen a ghost.

The billing clerk bolted out before Tanner could ask what kind of car Sheila or Julia drove to see if one of them had a muscle car.

If Julia was the kind of person she'd been made out to be, he doubted she would be caught dead in anything less than an expensive vehicle, like a top-of-the-line BMW or Mercedes. But then, nothing was out of the question here.

"She knew BethAnne was dead and was afraid to ask us questions when we visited the office today," Aimee pointed out as he put the gearshift in Drive.

"I have questions," he said.

"Same here," Aimee concurred. "Like, for instance, what did Julia know about BethAnne and her husband."

"And did she know about Sheila?" he continued.

"What if Dr. Carrol lied about knowing about the pregnancy?" Aimee asked.

"Would he tell his wife?"

"No," Aimee conceded. "He most definitely wouldn't."

"Unless Julia found out on her own," he said.

"Missy made it seem like rumors were flying about Dr. Carrol and BethAnne," Aimee said. "I'm no pregnancy expert but wouldn't my cousin have morning sickness or something like that? Wouldn't there be signs?"

"Signs that people who worked in an OB/GYN office would be all too keen to pick up on," he agreed. "I've heard stories of my aunt and mother throwing up at the smell of things they once enjoyed."

"BethAnne's co-workers are in a unique position to read the signs of pregnancy," Aimee said.

"They would probably keep watch on anyone spending time with the doctor too," he said. "Out of curiosity's sake if nothing else. Small towns like to be in each other's business. Sometimes it's a good thing, like when someone brings over soup to someone who is bedridden, and sometimes it's mean-spirited."

Aimee nodded. She got quiet like she did when she was in deep thought.

"What if Julia had spies at the office, as well?" Aimee asked when she finally spoke up. "But then, wouldn't she know her husband was stopping off at my cousin's house after work?"

"Not if he left his cell phone at the office," he reasoned. "I've heard of teenagers pulling stuff like that when their parents put those tracker apps on them, but it's strange to think of a grown person doing the same thing."

"I couldn't agree more, but then he was hiding a lot from his wife," Aimee pointed out. "Plus, I've never seen those trackers actually work out with someone who didn't want to be tracked. To your point, there are ways to get around it. I had a friend in Austin once who figured out how to block the app when they slept over, making it seem like we stayed in my room the whole night. Someone who is tech savvy can figure out a workaround like that." She snapped her fingers.

"I'd be interested to speak to his wife," he said.

"Maybe we should swing by the good doctor's house," she said. "Shake things up a little bit."

"And say what?"

"I have no problem pretending like I'm having an affair with the man, and that I wanted to check to see if he really had left his wife," she said.

"It could work," he reasoned. "It might also put you in harm's way if BethAnne was murdered for having an affair."

"She might have been murdered for becoming pregnant," Aimee said. "The pregnancy might have been the straw that broke the camel's back. A person like Julia couldn't have an illegitimate child out there if Missy's evaluation of the woman is accurate."

He nodded and then turned the wheel toward the good doctor's home. "There's a problem with this theory."

"I know," Aimee said. "It doesn't explain how a woman could be strong enough to strangle BethAnne from behind and then drag her body to the gravesite. Then, there's the part about BethAnne not having a viable pregnancy after all."

"Which doesn't necessarily mean she didn't tell her boyfriend she was pregnant," he said. "If Julia found out through her spies, they might not have known the fetus didn't have a chance."

"The pregnancy hadn't aborted yet, so that makes sense," she reasoned. "Do you know where the doctor lives?"

"One of the benefits of growing up in Lone Star Pass is that I know where all the prominent folks reside." He also knew where pretty much everyone else in town lived, having spent his entire life in the same town. He hadn't gone off to college like some of his friends, relatives, and classmates. He'd stayed back to work the ranch and then ended up caught up in all the family drama.

As much as he'd given Rowan a hard time for leaving recently, Tanner wished he could do the same.

"What if Julia isn't home?" Aimee asked.

"My mom has been transported to a jail in Houston," he said. "Looks like it's time to visit her if we can't find Julia here."

"We don't know where she lives," Aimee pointed out.

"And there's also the little problem of our visit to the doctor's home tipping him off to the fact we're looking for his wife," he said.

"Then, we'll come up with a good reason to visit him," she said, pausing for a few minutes. "I know."

He had a few ideas of his own but let her go first.

"I'll become hysterical about losing my cousin," she said. "I'll blame him for the murder, even if he didn't 'pull the trigger' so to speak, I'll say he's still responsible."

In Tanner's book, the man was as guilty as sin. If BethAnne had been murdered because of her affair with the doctor, he had blood on his hands. After visiting the office today, it was easy to see the man was a coward. Was he a murderer too?

Or would he not want to get his hands dirty?

"I could go into a rage," he offered. "It wouldn't be that big of a stretch for me, considering I'd like to take the bastard out back and have five minutes alone with him if he's responsible for BethAnne's murder."

Tanner wouldn't. He knew violence wasn't the answer.

"I think it's safer if I'm the one to do it," Aimee said. "The last thing we need is for you to end up in jail because you threatened the doctor. You're not exactly in the clear yourself so we don't want to give the sheriff any reason to arrest you." She softened her voice and said, "I wouldn't want to do any of this without you, Tanner."

His chest squeezed at those words. Because he couldn't imagine not having her by his side now or in the future.

∽

AIMEE PINCHED the bridge of her nose. It had been one helluva long day and it wasn't over yet. Time was of the essence. Besides, she was too wired to sleep anyway. Not when they were making progress, albeit inch by inch.

There was a popular hashtag in the workout community that was #brickbybrick. This felt the same. They were clawing for every inch of forward progress. But they were gaining ground and she wouldn't let a little thing like being tired get in the way of finding her cousin's killer. For all anyone knew, the murderer might be biding their time until they could strike again. Although, all signs pointed toward this being related to her affair.

The muscle car was the missing piece.

Okay, to be fair, there was more than one missing piece. She had a feeling the muscle car would lead them in the right direction.

"My heart is breaking for my aunt and uncle," she finally said.

"I can't imagine losing a daughter," he agreed. "Not that the pain would be any less if it was a son. Losing a child, even an adult one, has to be the worst possible pain imaginable."

"Do you want kids?" she asked, surprising herself with the question.

"I've never wanted them," Tanner said. "In fact, I've been solidly against the whole parenting gig until recently."

"Oh yeah? What changed?"

"Seeing my cousins and a few of my brothers become dads," he said as he navigated onto the highway. "Watching them get parenting right, not to mention seeing how happy their families have made them, has made me question my strong stance on the subject." He paused for a few beats. "What about you? Do you ever see yourself becoming a mother someday? Or is parenthood out of the question for you?"

"If you'd asked me this question last week, I would have had a solid answer," she shared. "To be clear, the answer would have been no. But after losing my cousin, who was the closest family member to me, I'm not so sure anymore." She didn't want to give away the red blush crawling up her neck, so she turned to look out the passenger window. "If I met the right person, I could see possibly changing my mind. It would take someone special, though."

She didn't dare risk a glance in his direction while feeling so vulnerable.

"You'd be an amazing mother if you ever decided to go down that road," he said with a confidence she didn't feel.

"What makes you say that?"

"You always looked after BethAnne," he said. "She talked about you all the time. About your kindness."

Aimee issued a sharp sigh. "I highly doubt the world would call me kind."

"You're strong too," he added, causing more of the heat to flame her cheeks. "I think people confuse strength with being hard sometimes but that's not true. I've seen you be kind to BethAnne's neighbor. I've also seen you be tough in the face of hard decisions. You stayed by BethAnne's side until she was taken out of that hole in the ground, refusing to leave even though your body trembled almost the entire time from being cold and wet. Most folks wouldn't do that."

"I couldn't leave her there with strangers," she reasoned, but his words were providing comfort.

"And then there's your aunt and uncle," he continued. "You're doing everything in your power to protect them during what has to be the most difficult time in their lives without any concern for yourself. In fact, you'd rather face something hard if it meant they didn't have to. Not many people would care that much."

"It's the right thing to do," she defended. What was it about receiving compliments that made her so uncomfortable? Didn't people usually love to be showered with them? They usually felt hollow to her, though, but coming from Tanner, they meant something. He wasn't the type to dole out compliments for no reason. She trusted him. "They didn't ask for any of this, and they lost the apple of their eye."

"You're always thinking of others and putting their needs first," he pointed out.

"With people I care about," she clarified.

"It goes deeper than that," he said. "I remember you found a baby squirrel once that was only a month old back when you used to come out to visit with your cousin. You called the vet and asked what to do before nursing the little thing until it could survive in the wild on its own a month later. If memory serves, you gave it a name. Rofurt, I believe."

"That doesn't count," she countered.

"Why not?"

"It was helpless," she said. "What kind of society would we be if we didn't protect things weaker than ourselves?"

"Not one that I would want to live it," he agreed, warming her heart. "It's a breath of fresh air."

"You act like this is the first time we've known each other," she said. "You do realize I spent quite a few of my summers here in Lone Star Pass."

"You were knee-high to a grasshopper back then," he pointed out. "And, basically, BethAnne's annoying younger cousin."

She turned in time to see him crack a smile. It broke some of the tension sitting thick in the air and provided a much-needed moment of respite from all the heavy emotions sitting on her shoulders like a thick, wet blanket.

"I had the biggest crush on you back then," she admitted with more than a little embarrassment.

"No way," he said, his smile widening.

"You can wipe that grin off your face, Tanner. I didn't say that I had a crush on you today."

"Why not?" he quipped in a playful tone that brought down more of the tension that had a chokehold on her after the visit to the sheriff's office.

"Because I grew up," she said without thinking. "Because childhood crushes don't last. Because you definitely weren't into me."

"How old are you?" he wasted no time in asking.

"Twenty-seven," she answered.

"I'm thirty-one," he pointed out. "That's a four-year difference. If I'd noticed you back in high school, that would have been a problem, don't you think?"

Well, that made her laugh.

"I guess so," she agreed. "The difference between a seventeen-year-old and a thirteen-year-old is a big gap."

"Not to mention an illegal one," he added. "Plus, when I was fifteen, that would have made you eleven."

"I got your drift," she said. "And you're right. You were quite the 'older man' to me back then."

"Four years isn't much now," he said and then seemed to catch himself. It was his turn to blush. And that made her feel more than a little smug.

He exited the highway and then turned into a fancy development with yards that are a few acres and million-dollar houses. It was the closest thing to a subdivision Aimee had seen in Lone Star Pass. "Is this new?"

"Yes," he said. "A developer came in a few years back and started building these McMansions for city folks who divide their time between here and San Antonio, Austin, and even Houston.

"This seems like the kind of neighborhood someone who comes from money would buy a house in," Aimee said.

"Most of those executives claim this as their permanent address to avoid taxes," he said. "Technically, this counts as farmland."

"Wealthy people and their tax shelters," she said with a headshake. "Too bad I don't have enough money to need to hide any of it for fear the government might take it away."

He laughed but she wondered if she struck a chord. It was easy to forget Tanner's family was one of the wealthiest in Texas.

"Sorry if I brought up a sensitive topic," she said. The last thing she wanted to do was hurt his feelings.

"Don't worry about it," he said.

"It's just easy to forget how loaded you are because you don't act rich," she said.

"The inheritance is new for me," he admitted. "But even if it wasn't, other than put food on the table and a roof over my head, I see no need for piles of cash sitting around in a bank account."

"Does that mean you'll give yours away?"

"No, not all of it," he answered honestly. "I've thought about ways in which I can help the community, but I needed time to adjust." He shook his head. "I'm sure that made no sense but what I'm trying to say is that I want to make sure I make a difference with it."

"That's noble."

"No one would accuse me of being a saint," he quipped.

"Sinners can be a whole lot more fun," she said with a laugh.

The smiles wiped from both of their faces as they pulled up to 1212 Mustang Court. Lights were out and the folks inside were about to get quite a wake-up call.

16

Tanner parked, exited the truck, and walked straight up to a set of massive wooden double doors. There was an ornate lion-headed doorknocker and a camera doorbell on the right-hand side. Having both was overkill if anyone asked him but they didn't. And, being completely honest, he knew the owners didn't care about his opinion one way or the other.

He rang the bell as Aimee took the knocker. The metal against metal sound echoed through the darkness.

Since this wasn't exactly a social call, Tanner rang the bell incessantly. Yes, he was being a nuisance. No, he wasn't concerned about it. A couple of odd thoughts crept in the back of his mind as he stood next to Aimee, waiting for the doctor or his wife to answer. The first was about the kiss they'd shared. He'd thought about that more than once in the past fourteen hours since it had happened. No one had ever awakened his senses in the way she had. He prided himself on being in control, and she threatened to obliterate his in a matter of seconds.

It was strange, because that had never happened to him before.

The other was his disappointment at her getting over her childhood crush on him. Why did that bother him? Did he want something more with Aimee? Or was it just his pride taking the wheel?

No answer at the door.

Aimee stood there with her arms crossed over her chest while she tapped the toe of her foot on the stones underfoot. "No one is this deep of a sleeper."

"Probably not," he agreed. "Which might mean his wife isn't home."

"Or he could be calling the sheriff, hiding on the other side of that door," she pointed out with disgust. "If I live to be a hundred years old, I'll never understand what my cousin saw in him."

"I'd rather keep the sheriff out of this," he reasoned. Bringing Lawler in might only make things worse. Although, the sheriff wasn't ready to dismiss Tanner as a suspect yet, which frustrated the hell out of him.

What would he have to gain by killing BethAnne?

Aimee knocked more aggressively this time. Tanner hit the bell, covering the camera with his hand. The bad news was there would be a recording of their visit. Even with his hand over the camera, it already caught them as they walked up and stood there. These kinds of doorbells were usually monitored by the resident or homeowner who, in turn, paid a monthly fee similar to the way Ring worked. The doorbell camera crazy had swept the nation and the evidence sent quite a few burglars behind bars.

It was odd to have one of these on a home in Lone Star Pass but then the town was no longer the safe haven it once was. Everyone had to be careful these days.

Aimee slammed the knocker again, and the door came open a crack. A disheveled Robert Carrol rubbed his eyes.

"What do you want?" he asked. "It's the middle of the night for God's sake."

"We're here to speak to your wife," Aimee said.

"What? Why?" He shook his head like he was trying to shake off sleep fog. "She's not here."

"Where can we find her?" Aimee pressed.

"In Houston," he said, but he didn't sound convincing. Did he know where his wife was at present?

"How long has it been since she's been home?" Aimee asked, leaning closer to Robert. Ready to stick her toe in the door if he decided to close it on them?

Tanner had to hand it to her, she was savvy. Not much got past her. She was also determined and he figured she was pushing outside her comfort zone to find answers about her cousin.

"It's her month to be in Houston," he said in a tone that made it seem like all spouses took these kinds of breaks from each other.

"Is she there every other month?" Aimee continued.

"Yes, usually," he said. "But it depends on what she has going on there."

"I didn't think she had a job," Aimee said.

"It's all charity work," he supplied. "She's involved in the mayor's ball and several charities bringing the arts to Houston. Why?"

"I wanted to ask her a few questions about her relationship with my cousin," Aimee said point-blank.

"Why would y—"

He stopped the minute he figured out where Aimee was going with this. He shook his head. "My wife wouldn't hurt a flea."

Even if that was true, which Tanner couldn't say one way or the other, Robert's body language said something else. His gaze shot up and to the right which meant he was most likely lying. Covering? Did he suspect his wife might have found out about his affairs?

Still, she didn't fit the profile of the person Tanner believed they were looking for. Her absence, however, explained why Tanner didn't run into her the rare times he had to do something in town. Most supplies were delivered to the ranch rather than needing to be picked up, but he made his way into town once in a blue moon.

"Mind if we take a look around your home?" Tanner finally spoke up.

Robert stared at Tanner for a long moment before finally taking a step back and saying, "Why not? I've got nothing to hide."

The move surprised Tanner and gave the doctor a little more credibility in Tanner's book. The saying, *you don't get what you don't ask for*, came to mind. Tanner was glad that he'd asked.

Robert took a step back after opening the door wide. He had on pajamas and a robe that was open in the front with the tie hanging at his sides.

"Do you, by chance, have any rope in the garage?" Tanner asked, figuring he might as well go for it.

"I'm sure there's something in there but I'm not a handyman, so I couldn't say for sure," Robert said, rubbing his eyes again as he yawned.

"This would be a specific kind of rope we're looking for," Tanner clarified.

Robert's eyebrows drew together in confusion. And then it seemed to dawn on him what Tanner might be referring to when his eyes widened. "Oh. Damn. Okay. What type would that be?"

"Like the kind used at ranches or at the rodeo," Tanner informed the doctor, who subconsciously brought his hand up to his neck and rubbed.

Robert shook his head. "I wouldn't rule anything out since I don't do the work around here. The only time I go into the garage is to get inside my car or when I'm coming home. But I highly doubt you'll find anything like that in there." He shrugged. "It's worth a look, though. Follow me and we'll figure it out together."

"Who does the work around here if not you?" Aimee asked.

"I'm afraid my wife handles everything that has to do with our homes," Robert said as he led them down a hallway that could fit most one-bedroom apartments with space to spare.

"How does she pay workers?" Aimee asked.

"Could be writing them checks for all I know," he said on another shrug. They crossed through a massive kitchen that looked spit-shined and like brand new. Tanner doubted Julia Carrol did a whole lot of her own cooking based on what he'd been told about her so far. "Okay, let's see what we have in here."

A light automatically turned on as Robert opened the door to his four-car garage. His Range Rover sat at the opposite end along with a customized Mercedes. One of the bays was empty, that had to be the vehicle Julia had with her in Houston. And then there was an Audi Q7. It was quite an impressive array of vehicles.

The back wall was covered in floor-to-ceiling cabinets, painted black.

"Be my guest," Robert said, motioning toward the row as he started opening doors.

Tanner took the far end and worked toward Aimee in the middle. Robert took the ones closest to the door.

Two cabinets in, Tanner stopped. "Hey, come over here and look at this."

"What is it?" Aimee asked.

Tanner caught her gaze and held it. "Rope fibers."

∼

AIMEE GASPED. "You know what this means?"

"Someone on this property had the same kind of rope that strangled BethAnne," Tanner confirmed what they both already knew.

"Which doesn't mean it's from the same rope," Aimee pointed out.

"Didn't the sheriff say there were clothing fibers mixed in?" Tanner asked, stepping away from the opened cabinet.

"Yes, as a matter of fact, he did." Aimee didn't think Robert was guilty despite the lame fishing alibi. Had he most likely moved on to his next conquest? That seemed like the most logical explanation. This seemed like a good time to ask. "Who else have you been sleeping with at the office?"

"No one," Robert said with a disgusted look. Seriously?

"Are you telling me that you haven't moved on from my cousin? That you didn't already line up your next conquest before the sheets were cold?"

Robert stood there for a long moment, staring her down. "I'm not sleeping with anyone who works at my office. Period."

Aimee realized she wasn't asking the right question. "What about someone who doesn't work for you?"

The man looked guilty as sin. He was sleeping with someone. Did BethAnne find out about the other woman? Was that the reason she'd been so withdrawn lately?

Of course, she wouldn't have wanted to admit to sleeping with a married man if she figured out Robert was lying to her. With his wife gone every other month, it would be easier to convince BethAnne he was single or soon-to-be at least.

Robert issued a sharp sigh. He paced a couple of laps around the empty space in his garage. "You're going to find out anyway, so I might as well tell you." He stopped talking long enough to shoot a look of apology.

"There's a drug rep who I've been dating on and off for a year now," he said. "We've been planning to get married once I get a divorce from Julia."

"You don't have to feed us that line, Robert," Tanner piped in. "Neither one of us is trying to sleep with you."

"It's not a line," he said defensively. "Sarah Pippen is her name. I love her and I want to build a future together." He put his right hand in the air palm out. "That's the honest truth."

"Does she know about BethAnne?" Tanner asked. He was onto something there. If Sarah believed her future was in jeopardy, she might become desperate enough to kill to protect what she believed to be hers.

"No," Robert said.

"I think you're naïve if you really believe the folks in your office don't notice everything and speak to one another," Aimee pointed out.

"No one knows about Sarah," he said.

"I wouldn't be too certain about that," Aimee countered. "They knew about Sheila."

"I was sloppy, dating her at work," he admitted like that was his biggest misstep and not the fact he was cheating on his wife. No matter how bad a marriage might be, no one deserved to be cheated on. Do yourself and your partner a favor...get the divorce. "It was a mistake to go about it the way I did."

Aimee folded her arms across her chest. "Can I ask you a question?"

Robert nodded.

"Why get married at all?" she asked. "I mean, why not live a single life and sleep with whoever you want to, without hurting anyone else because it's clear to me that you didn't actually mean your vows?"

"Julia doesn't want a divorce," Robert said, like that absolved all his bad behavior, like that put him in the clear and made his actions Julia's fault instead of taking responsibility for his actions. "I hinted at one and she said there was no way she was taking that hit. We agreed to a loose marriage."

"Open marriage?" Tanner clarified.

"Whatever," Robert said. "Except that I was supposed to be discreet about it. Then, I met Sarah and we fell in love."

Aimee highly doubted the man knew the true meaning of the word love. The whole *in sickness and in health* and *for richer or for poorer* seemed lost on the man. He had made those vows to Julia, like it or not. "What about BethAnne?"

He shook his head. "I had feelings, of course; but she was clear that our 'arrangement' was temporary."

Aimee couldn't prove the slimeball was lying despite how much the little voice inside her head screamed the words.

"Anyway, things heated up between Sarah and I, so we decided to take some time apart until I could figure out how to break it off with Julia. My wife is a stubborn woman who is used to getting everything she wants," he said. Again, like that explained everything and gave him a free pass to sleep around. Jerk wasn't nearly big enough a word to describe this man.

"But that's not what you told BethAnne," Aimee said.

"How do you know?" Robert asked.

"Because my cousin wouldn't have slept with you if she didn't have feelings for you, and she never would have allowed herself to have feelings for you if she thought you were staying with your wife or in love with someone else," Aimee explained, trying to keep her blood pressure from hitting the roof. She wanted this bastard to feel some of the pain he inflicted on unsuspecting women.

"And then there's Sheila to consider," Tanner added, arms crossed, leaning against a cabinet door.

"How did you find out about her, by the way?" Robert asked.

"The office knows about her," Aimee said. "This is a small town. Do you really think your sexual appetite hasn't hit the rumor mill by now?"

He shot a look that said he hadn't considered the possibility.

What? Did he think he was being that sneaky?

"Where did you leave things with Sarah?" Tanner asked, bringing the conversation back on track.

"The last time we spoke, I told her it wouldn't be much longer until we could be together," Robert confessed. "I told her that I had to wrap up a few details here with Julia and that we'd be married before she knew it."

"Did you plan to marry her?" Aimee asked, figuring it

was a question worth asking with his past. It was taking all her self-discipline not to lambaste this poor excuse for a human being.

"At some point," he said. "Yes."

"Is that who you were with the other night, when you were supposed to be on a fishing trip?" Tanner asked.

"No, because she never showed up," Robert said. And then his eyes widened like he'd just put two-and-two together.

Sarah might be responsible for BethAnne's murder. She had to know that Robert would lie for her if she asked him to, and say she was with him at the fishing cabin. And he would have if he truly loved her, which he probably believed he did love her. His kind of love was broken, bad, and hurt others.

Real love meant sacrifice, which Aimee highly doubted this man had the guts to do. Not with the way he manipulated women. It made Aimee sick to her stomach to know there were slimeballs like him out there preying on people's loneliness.

He'd been right about one thing, BethAnne had been lonely.

She'd been holding out for Tanner to come to his senses and finally see her as something other than a friend. To break down the pact they'd made years ago because he realized he'd always been in love with her like some fairy tale version of life.

After spending time together, Aimee realized that was never going to happen. It was obvious Tanner cherished his friendship with BethAnne, but it was abundantly clear he would never see her as more. Unlike the class-A jerk doctor, Tanner had truly been upfront about where he stood. BethAnne had been living in a made-up version of reality, hoping he would come to his senses like they were in one of those rom-com movies she loved to watch after a few rounds of margaritas.

"You have to go to Sheriff Lawler and tell him everything you just told us," Aimee said, point-blank. She was giving him no other option. This was his way out to redeem himself and prove he wasn't the lowest scum walking the earth. "He has been barking up the wrong tree and needs to be set straight. By you. You know all the background. It has to come from your mouth."

"He'd arrest me on the spot," Robert whined. "Where would that leave my medical practice, not to mention my marriage?"

"Since when have you been concerned about Julia?" Aimee asked, feeling bad for being so hard on his wife before. More than a twinge of guilt hit.

"I can't bring that kind of shame down on her," Robert said, starting to sound desperate. "No one can know about the affairs."

"Too late," Tanner said, holding up his cell phone. "I've recorded this entire conversation. You will go to the sheriff, and you're going tonight."

Tanner took a step toward Robert, and then the lights went out. The room was pitch black and Aimee couldn't see her hand in front of her face.

17

Tanner crouched low, in case the person who shut off the light had a weapon and decided to shoot. A bullet to one of the gas tanks wouldn't cause an explosion but broken glass could cut them. They could be hit with bullet fragments or, of course, the bullet itself.

Robert hadn't been standing anywhere near the light switch, so it couldn't possibly have been him. There'd been two other folks in the garage to Tanner's knowledge, both him and Aimee.

So, who the hell joined the party?

Asking wasn't an option, because he didn't want to give away his position as he made his way over to where he'd last seen Aimee standing. He had to consider the fact she might be on the move too. Logic said she might be trying to get to him. Bumping into each other would draw unwanted attention.

"What the hell?" Robert asked, panic in his voice. "Who cut off the damn light?" He muttered a string of curses that would make any Southern grandma wash his mouth out with soap.

Thankfully, Aimee had enough sense not to vocalize a response. Rather, he put a hand out in front of him as he crouched low and 'walked' while he searched for her. Found her hunkered down behind the Range Rover.

The sound of Robert spamming the switch echoed in the large garage. Someone must have turned off the lights via the breaker switch. That someone would have to know their way around the place. Was it Julia, his wife? Or had he brought Sarah to his home?

Tanner wondered if Robert would be that obvious since there was a camera at the front door. Possibly others. Then again, there was always a workaround when it came to technology. There were always blind spots. Robert could have brazenly brought his mistress home in his Range Rover, walked her straight inside.

What did the person who cut off the lights intend to do with all three of them? Killing them would leave an awfully high body count.

Then again, desperate folks did desperate things. He needed to get Aimee out of here and far away, preferably before the lights flipped back on or the person responsible figured out where they were.

The glow from a cell phone flashlight illuminated a face. A female cursed. There was definitely another woman in the garage. But the light went off before he could get a good look at her. Julia or Sarah were his two best guesses.

What did she plan to do?

He tugged at Aimee's arm, indicating she should follow him. She kept a hand on his back as he crouched low and walked toward the door. It was the only exit he knew other than trying to pull up a garage door by hand, which may or may not work. The best he could do would be get them back to the door leading into the hallway from the kitchen into the home. Not ideal. He also realized he left the Colt .45 inside his truck. The doors of his vehicle were locked at least. If he could get to his truck, he could grab his gun. They wouldn't be defenseless any longer.

Although he saw a female's face, he had no idea how many others there might be around aiding Julia or Sarah. Didn't Robert say something about a workman who regularly took care of the home and lawn?

Julia could have solicited him to help her. Tanner's mother had used others to attempt to pull off her scheme to get and keep more of the Firebrand family fortune. It was a tactic that had almost worked.

Staying low to the floor, he managed to get them to the door by moving around the perimeter.

"Who is here?" Robert asked, a little more panicked this time. "What are you doing? This is my home, dammit. Show yourself or leave right now." His attempt to sound authoritative fell flat.

Out of nowhere, a thud sounded. A car alarm followed. Robert screamed at the top of his lungs, his voice could be heard above the screech.

"Get off me," he shouted. "Stop." A choking noise tore from his throat. "Stop." He managed to repeat the word a couple of times.

Whoever was attacking him had to know Tanner and Aimee were here. His truck was out front. It had the Firebrand logo on a sticker. There'd be no mistaking it. Was someone bold enough to kill Robert with witnesses in the room?

Did this person believe they would actually get away with murder and just walk a—

Hold on. Whoever had attacked Robert had no intention of leaving the witnesses. Since the lights were cut from a source outside of the garage, there'd be no turning them back on.

Desperate times called for desperate measures.

Tanner reached for the doorknob. Found it. He was two seconds away from escape with Aimee. But leaving Robert behind to die would haunt Tanner for the rest of his life when he could do something about it. So, he wouldn't.

He pulled Aimee close to him and then whispered in her ear. "Stay here and stay low. Okay?"

She put his hand on her face, and then nodded.

Tanner palmed his key, remembering he could hit the emergency alarm if he needed to create a distraction If the piercing alarm in the garage stopped even with his truck parked out front. Holding the key in his hand would also give him a little extra mass if he had to throw a punch.

He fished his cell out of his pocket with his free hand, and then let his thumb hover over the flashlight feature. The light could be blinding if aimed directly at the eyes. It could give him a couple seconds of advantage.

So many questions flooded his brain. Would Julia be strong enough to throw Robert against the vehicle? Would Sarah? Was there more than one person in the garage orchestrating this...whatever *this* was.

Alright, standing around contemplating the situation wasn't solving anything. It was go time.

The sound of a bullet split the air, but he couldn't focus on that right now. Instead, he tapped the light feature on his cell and gained his bearings. A man had Robert sprawled over the hood of the vehicle with an elbow at his throat. Robert was losing the fight as his arms and legs flailed in different directions. Robert was no match.

Tanner cut off the light and dove toward the burly dude on top of Robert. The second after he made contact, his cell went flying. The noise from the alarm made it impossible to hear his own thoughts let alone approximately where the cell landed.

How long would the alarm go off? It was splitting his head in two, making holding a thought next to impossible.

Tanner landed on the burly dude, knocking him off Robert. This probably wasn't the time to regret not calling 911 before he made the leap, but it was too late now. Would Aimee think to do it? He tried to shout over the alarm and failed. He couldn't hear himself. There was no way she would be able to.

The next thing he knew, he was body-slammed into the hard flooring after skidding off the hood. Robert coughed. The sound was reassuring that Tanner had made it in time before Robert had been choked to death. Tanner bucked the large dude off him and fought for control.

The woman he assumed to be Julia—because she was the only one who would know the layout of the home like the back of her hand—was somewhere in the garage. She had the advantage of knowing this place, whereas Tanner and Aimee were flying blind. He'd had enough time to memorize the basic layout.

Burly Dude twisted around and somehow managed to come out on top. Tanner was pinned by the dude, who had to weigh two-hundred-plus pounds, give or take. Twisting like a snake to confuse Burly Dude, the whizz of a punch sounded next to Tanner's ear, connecting with the concrete flooring. Burly Dude cried out in pain.

Tanner took advantage of the momentary weakness by bucking Burly Dude off. Over the piercing alarm, Tanner heard the dude grunt. One of the dude's body parts slammed into the vehicle with a thud. His head? His shoulder?

Tanner threw a kick, connected with a leg or knee. It was impossible to hear over the siren.

And then lights flipped on. The door opened. Sheriff Lawler appeared at the doorway with his weapon drawn and shouted, "Hands up where I can see 'em. I'm talking to every single person in this room." A sliver of the sheriff's face could be seen as he used the doorframe and wall as a barrier.

Two deputies flanked the doorway in a similar fashion. Tanner could see enough of one of them to realize they had on bulletproof vests. They did not come to mess around. The sheriff and his deputies were prepared to handle a small army.

The car alarm stopped after the lights flashed and a final guttural noise sounded.

Aimee sat against the wall, phone in hand, blood on her left arm and shoulder. The bullet? Had she been shot?

Panic nearly crippled him as he made a move to get to her, but nothing was going to stop him from crossing the room. Not the burly bastard. Not the law. Not Robert.

"Don't move," one of the deputies ordered with a threatening voice. Too late. Tanner was already rushing to her side.

"Aimee's been shot," was all he could say. He put his hands in the air but he kept going while the others in the garage froze.

There was so much blood. Too much. Aimee's face had turned bleached-sheet white, and her lips were blue. The mere possibility of losing her ripped his heart out. Not now. Not ever.

Tanner finally understood what his brother had been trying to tell him. Love decided when it would strike. The best anyone could do was hold onto it if they were lucky enough to find someone they didn't couldn't ever see themselves living without.

"Aimee," he said, dropping down to her side as she shot him a look of apology.

"I got in the way of the bullet," she said, her eyes fluttering as she winced. "I'm sorry."

"No need to apologize," Tanner reassured despite his heart being ripped from his chest. "You'll be okay." It was a promise he knew full well that he might not be able to keep. Yet, he would give his right arm if it would make a difference. "Show me where you're hit."

Aimee tried to move but gestured toward her shoulder.

"Set your weapon down on the floor," Sheriff Lawler demanded as Tanner shrugged out of his flannel shirt and then his t-shirt. He balled up the white t, and then used it to stem the bleeding. He managed to get his flannel back on, unbuttoned.

From the corner of his eye, he saw what was going on with Julia. She seemed to know better than to tempt fate with the lawman. She studied him for a long moment before finally bending down and placing the gun on the floor.

"I need an ambulance over here," Tanner shouted as the shirt he used to put pressure on the shoulder wound became soaked with her blood.

"Kick the weapon over toward me," Sheriff Lawler instructed, leaving no room for argument in his tone while acknowledging Tanner with a nod.

"We need that ambulance, Sheriff," Tanner pleaded. "There's no time to waste."

Aimee's eyes rolled back in their sockets, then closed as her head dropped to one side.

"No. No. No." Tanner let go of the balled-up bloody shirt

to hold her head upright. He mumbled a string of curses as a hand reached inside his chest and fisted around his heart. "Don't go, Aimee."

Aimee was unresponsive.

He immediately checked for a pulse. If one was there, it was faint.

"We need help over here," he pleaded with the sheriff.

Lawler nodded to one of his deputies, who came jogging over as sirens sounded in the background.

"Help is on the way," the deputy said as he picked up the shirt, balled it up, and reapplied pressure.

Tanner hoped like hell the EMTs wouldn't be too late.

"Stay with me."

Tanner's voice broke through the fog and made Aimee fight harder to stay awake. She blinked her eyes open to the best sight…him. He locked gazes with her.

"You're going to be alright," he promised. "Do you understand me?"

She wanted to speak, to say yes, but exhaustion was an overwhelming force. Could she tell him that she would be fine once she got some rest?

"No. No. No."

The sound of panic in his voice jolted her back to the present.

"Wake up," he urged.

"Okay," she managed to say on an exhale. Her head rolled to the side and she saw blood. Her blood. "It's cold."

The next thing she knew, Tanner peeled off his flannel shirt and draped it over her like a blanket.

"Please," he said to someone off to the side. "We need that ambulance. Tell them to hurry."

The last thing she saw before she drifted off was his beautiful face. "I love you, Tanner."

Everything went dark.

~

Panic gripped Aimee. She forced her eyes open and sat bolt upright. Gentle hands were suddenly guiding her back down.

"Hey there," Tanner said in almost a whisper, his tone a mix of anguish and relief. Hearing his voice brought a wave of warmth along with a sense of calm washing over her. "You're in the hospital and you're going to be fine. You've been out of it for two days."

She glanced around the room, confirming what he'd already told her. The beige walls and sterile white tile flooring were pretty good indicators of where she was.

It took a second to remember what happened, but the memories came crashing down when she did.

"Robert?" she managed to ask through a scratchy throat.

"He's fine," Tanner confirmed as he located a large drinking cup with a straw. He helped her take a few sips, which immediately started to ease some of the dryness. "He's a cheating bastard, but he's alright."

She sighed in relief. The last thing she remembered was him lying across the hood of a vehicle being choked out, while its alarm cut through her brain.

"Julia?"

"In jail," Tanner stated with a hint of satisfaction. "Turns out she threatened to have Pablo deported if he didn't help her get rid of 'the problem', which was only supposed to be BethAnne's child. Robert lied about the open marriage. Julia knew nothing of the kind. In fact, she was planning to start their family, which is the reason she needed BethAnne and the baby to go away. She lured BethAnne to the park by slipping a fake note from her husband onto her windshield. The note promised he'd figured out a way for the two of them to be together."

Aimee eased to sitting as Tanner grabbed onto her hand and linked their fingers. A few tears leaked from her eyes at the thought someone could be so ruthless as to murder her sweet cousin for a mistake she never intended to make. BethAnne had clearly gotten swept up in Robert's charms and lost her life because of it.

"Some people are truly evil," she said. "What is going to happen to Pablo?"

"He'll be jailed after he testifies against his former employer," he informed. "Once he serves his time, he'll be deported."

"Doesn't seem fair on the one hand, except my cousin is gone and can never come back because he went along with Julia's demands," Aimee said, awash in mixed emotions.

"If he'd stopped at some point along the way and gone to the law, this would be a different outcome," Tanner pointed out. "He is remorseful for killing BethAnne but didn't think he had a choice since his family depends on him to bring money home. Without him, he believes they'll starve."

"Still, he murdered my cousin," she said. "It's difficult to feel sorry for him."

"I know," Tanner agreed. "It's just a bad situation all around."

She nodded. "Why kill BethAnne, though? She lost the pregnancy."

"No one knew that," he stated. "Especially not Julia.

Sheila is the one who came to Julia to tell her about BethAnne's pregnancy. It was a form of revenge for the doctor moving on so fast to someone else."

"What a jerk move," Aimee said. If Sheila had been able to keep her mouth shut, BethAnne might still be alive. The doctor had already moved on to Sarah.

"This situation gets even more twisted," Tanner said. "As it turns out, Julia's six weeks pregnant."

"Doesn't seem fair to the child to be born in prison," Aimee said. "But it serves Julia right, not to ever be able to have the family she thought she deserved and was willing to kill for, even if it was a façade."

"Robert said he would fight for full custody. He and Sarah plan to raise the baby together. He wasn't lying about making plans to marry her and now seems to have a good reason to speed up the timeline."

Aimee made a disgusted face. "Maybe he'll be able to keep his pants up this time."

"We can only hope he learned a valuable lesson," Tanner agreed. He paused and his face twisted in pain. "I thought I lost you there for a second." He clasped their hands a little tighter before bringing the back of hers up to his mouth. He pressed a tender kiss there.

"I'm right here," she reassured. "I'm not going anywhere unless you tell me to."

"You said something back in the garage," he hedged. "Do you remember?"

"Did I say it out loud?" she asked, thinking she'd kept that to her inner monologue.

"What do you think you said?"

"I love you, Tanner."

"And you meant it?" He studied her.

"Every word."

"Good because I haven't been able to think about anything else since," he admitted. "I've fallen in love with you, Aimee. I don't want to be without you for even a minute."

"Have you been here the whole time?"

"The only way I'm walking away from you is if that's what you want," he said with surprising vulnerability in his tone. "I'm in love with you. I'm at your mercy. Tell me to stay and I promise never to leave you."

Tears welled in Aimee's eyes. "I'd like that very much, Tanner Firebrand. I love you too. You're the person I want to share my every day with. The exciting. The boring. The everything that makes up a life. I never thought I'd want to get married or have a family. Turns out, I was just waiting for you all along without knowing it."

Tanner kissed her hand so tenderly it robbed her breath.

"I couldn't have said it better myself," he said. "And when you're ready, I plan to ask for your hand in marriage."

"What are you waiting for?" she asked. "If I've learned anything, it's how fast life can be taken away. I'm done wasting time. I want to spend the rest of my life with you. Ask me to marry you whenever you want. The answer is always going to be yes."

"I've been living at Firebrand Ranch my entire life, but it wasn't until you that I found home."

Aimee smiled at the man she'd fallen head over heels for. Because he wasn't the only one who'd found home.

18

EPILOGUE

Keith Firebrand wasn't in the mood to sing. If he was, he'd belt out Queen's *Another One Bites the Dust*. His brothers were falling like pins at the bowling alley, with Tanner the most recent victim...or...groom-to-be. What the hell was in the air causing them to fall in love?

The *must be something in the well water* jokes were getting out of hand at this point. Three single men were left standing out of a total of eighteen siblings and cousins. Keith, Travis, and Kellan were the lone wolves, holding onto their freedom like an eagle spreads its wings to fly.

The oldest brother, Kellan, was as likely to get married again as a bird was likely to sit down to eat a steak dinner. Wasn't happening. Travis was just as stubborn. There was hope he wouldn't trip down the aisle anytime soon, which left Keith. He was as likely to wed as snow during a Texas summer.

Hell would freeze over before either one of those things happened.

Besides, wheels were in motion. With all the mess going

on at Firebrand and Lone Star Pass, Keith realized how important it was to make his own way in life. Step away from his birthright at the ranch and start his own business. This place was beyond screwed up between the inheritance business and his mother's arrest. No matter how much his cousins pretended they didn't blame Keith's entire side of the family for their murderous mother, no one was *that* good.

Keith put himself in their shoes and couldn't honestly say he'd be able to forgive and forget as his cousins were planning to do. This side of the Firebrand family tree was headed up by greed and destruction. Granted, what his aunt and uncle had done to his cousin Brax was unthinkable, lying about his mother and pretending he was Aunt Lucia's child for all these years. There were other issues too, but the other side of the family seemed to have worked everything out. They were acting like a real family should, having cookouts with their new wives and, in some cases, children.

Meanwhile, Keith's side was still reeling from the actions of their mother. Their father was only incrementally better, having tried to run the wife of one of Keith's cousins out of town and done his fair share of crappy things.

As the youngest on either side of the family, Keith always had to shout to be heard. He'd spent a good portion of his life trying to get everyone to listen to reason, to him.

Now?

He was ready to leave all this behind and strike out on his own despite loving the land more than life itself. With this land came drama. Someone else's drama that he couldn't shake free of.

So, he'd put out word of his security and protection business. Much to his surprise, his first client was on the way and wanted his services in exchange for using 'an important person's name' as the caller had explained. The name of the person he was about to receive in order to protect was shrouded in secrecy. All he knew for certain was that she was some kind of internet celebrity. If he had a name, he would have researched her to see what he was about to get himself into. As it was, he was going into the situation blind.

This might not be the way he envisioned going into business for himself, but when opportunity knocked—or in this case called—he figured this was as good a time as any to jump in and get his feet wet.

Doing this would answer the question that had been eating away at him for months...years if he was being honest.

Did he truly belong at the only home he'd ever known?

Keep reading Keith's story here.

ALSO BY BARB HAN

Texas Firebrand

Rancher to the Rescue

Disarming the Rancher

Rancher under Fire

Rancher on the Line

Undercover with the Rancher

Rancher in Danger

Set-Up with the Rancher

Rancher Under the Gun

Taking Cover with the Rancher

Firebrand Cowboys

VAUGHN: Firebrand Cowboys

RAFE: Firebrand Cowboys

MORGAN: Firebrand Cowboys

NICK: Firebrand Cowboys

ROWAN: Firebrand Cowboys

TANNER: Firebrand Cowboys

KEITH: Firebrand Cowboys

Don't Mess With Texas Cowboys

Texas Cowboy's Protection

Texas Cowboy Justice

Texas Cowboy's Honor

Texas Cowboy Daddy

Texas Cowboy's Baby

Texas Cowboy's Bride

Texas Cowboy's Family

Texas Cowboy Sheriff

Texas Cowboy Marshal

Texas Cowboy Lawman

Texas Cowboy Officer

Texas Cowboy K9 Patrol

Cowboys of Cattle Cove

Cowboy Reckoning

Cowboy Cover-up

Cowboy Retribution

Cowboy Judgment

Cowboy Conspiracy

Cowboy Rescue

Cowboy Target

Cowboy Redemption

Cowboy Intrigue

Cowboy Ransom

For more of Barb's books, visit www.BarbHan.com.

ABOUT THE AUTHOR

Barb Han is a USA TODAY and Publisher's Weekly Bestselling Author. Reviewers have called her books "heartfelt" and "exciting."

Barb lives in Texas—her true north—with her adventurous family, a poodle mix, and a spunky rescue who is often referred to as a hot mess. She is the proud owner of too many books (if there is such a thing). When not writing, she can be found exploring new cities, on a mountain either hiking or skiing depending on the season, or swimming in her own backyard.

Sign up for Barb's newsletter at www.BarbHan.com.

Printed in Great Britain
by Amazon